THE
HAND
of REFUGE

THE
HAND
of REFUGE

ANTHONY CARTER

TATE PUBLISHING
AND ENTERPRISES, LLC

Published by Tate Publishing & Enterprises, LLC
127 E. Trade Center Terrace | Mustang, Oklahoma 73064 USA
1.888.361.9473 | www.tatepublishing.com

Tate Publishing is committed to excellence in the publishing industry. The company reflects the philosophy established by the founders, based on Psalm 68:11,
"The Lord gave the word and great was the company of those who published it."

Book design copyright © 2014 by Tate Publishing, LLC. All rights reserved.
Cover design by Errol Villamante
Interior design by Mary Jean Archival

Published in the United States of America

ISBN: 978-1-62746-851-0
1. Fiction / Christian / General
2. Fiction / General
14.03.07

For my wife Ashley, who was there when God had had enough of my doubts.

1 Corinthians 8:5–6 (KJV)

Chapter One

The Daily Herald

Washington, DC

"Excuse me, Ms. O'Neal? Mr. Birchen would like to see you in his office."

Cassandra looked up from her desk and fixed her hazel eyes on the editor in chief's assistant. She was not sure if she heard the woman right, but she could have sworn that she said Hal wanted to see her. That couldn't have been right, though. Hal knew she was swamped. They talked not even an hour ago about all of the revisions that she had to do on Jackson's and Carlyle's articles. He knew how pressed for time she was.

"Sorry, did you say Mr. Birchen wants to see me?"

The assistant nodded. "Yes, he's waiting for you in his office."

"Do you know what it's about?"

"No, he just asked me to let you know."

Cassandra nodded and thanked her. Then she saved the article on her computer screen and got up to see what Hal wanted. After leaving her office, she navigated the cubicles that dominated the center of the twenty-seventh floor and flashed a warm smile to everyone that she passed. She knew that she had too much to do and not enough time to do it all, so she did her best to not get caught up in any conversations.

"Hey, Cass'," said Julio. "Did you get the e-mail from Hal?"

Cassandra slowed to let the other editor catch up. "Not that I know of, why?"

"Have you even checked your mail?"

"Not in the last half-hour."

"You should check your in-box to see if you got it, I just finished reading it."

"Okay, I am on my way to talk to him now, so I will ask him about it," she said and turned to resume her journey to Hal's office.

"Oh, okay. I see," said Julio as he shook his head. "You still don't have time to talk to me. Whatever I did to you, I'm sorry."

Cassandra didn't want to be rude or crass but not everyone understood that there were deadlines to be met. Julio was one of those people who did not understand. He was a great guy and a lot of fun to be around, but he had a distinct advantage that none of the other editors had. He could read at a speed that was beyond anything a fast reader could hope to read at, and he had a gift with zeroing in on errors. He was always done well before the articles were due. and he was usually trying to get the next one from the writers as they were working on it. He didn't ever have to worry about not getting everything done like she did nor would he have to deal with how it would feel to make Hal and the paper look bad if time was wasted.

"Julio, it's not like that, I still have a lot to do and I don't have time to talk about the e-mail," she said. "Let's talk later, when I'm not caught up."

"Whatever," he said. "You've been in a funk for so long now that it's like the Cassandra I was friends with isn't even here anymore."

Cassandra did not know what to say to that. Even if she had a response, she didn't have a chance to voice it because Julio turned around and headed back to his office. She felt so bad. Yet, it was not her fault. Why couldn't he see that she was busy and that she didn't have time? It was frustrating.

She also knew that if she had an attitude it was not Julio's fault. Her problem was meeting the deadlines and trying to wade through the article that Geoff Jackson wrote. She thought a lot of Geoff; he was funny and brilliant in his own eccentric way. He was an excellent writer who had a knack for finding great stories that he infused with a lot of wit and humor. She cried and laughed as she read the works he dropped on her desk.

However, one of the problems that she and the other editors had with Geoff was that he did not use any commas, ever. When she talked to him about it, he said that commas and semicolons slowed him down. She had not had the heart to tell him that the on-going joke among some of the editors was that the key on his keyboard was broken. One of them had even believed it and decided to get him a new keyboard in the hope that commas would suddenly appear. When it did not work, they tasked her with editing all of his articles.

What perplexed Cassandra was why out of the three editors that Geoff worked with before her, none of them ever asked him why he didn't use commas or semicolons? They got a big laugh at his expense, which she found appalling. Yet, he got an ergonomic keyboard at one of theirs. It was about an even trade-off if suffering the shallowness of others could be considered a tradeoff, she thought.

Other issues with Geoff ran the gauntlet of never using apostrophes in the right place or context, capitalizing words that he considered to be 'names' that were not proper nouns, and at times being a bit redundant. Grammatical rules did not matter to him. He wanted to get the story down, get it off his desk and onto someone else's, and then get to the next story. It didn't matter to him if he capitalized police officer or not, so long as the article was written. Only, it did matter to the paper.

The door to the editor in chief's office was open as Cassandra approached it. She remembered when the office and title used to intimidate her but that had been in her days fresh out of college. Without bothering to knock, Cassandra barged in and looked at Hal through squinted eyelashes. His light green eyes had a startled glint in them that she did not see all that often; and his cheeks blushed beneath the close-cropped salt and pepper beard that he wore.

"Good to see you, too," he said. "Close the door and take a seat if you don't mind."

Cassandra crossed her arms and maintained her squint. "What is this about? You know I have a lot to do."

"Don't give me that angry façade. Just close the door and sit down, all right?"

Cassandra caved and did as he asked. The leather chair that she sat down in felt so much more comfortable than the office chair she used. If she could have gotten away with it, she would have swapped her own for Hal's, but there were limits to his patience with her. The chair would have reeked of the cologne he wore, though. It was the essence of Old Man she had once quipped, to which he shot back the French designer's name and how expensive it was. It did not matter what name was attached to it, she still believed that he should demand a refund.

"So, what makes you pull me from the editing that I have to get done before I leave?"

Hal smiled. "I have been doing some thinking and I was wondering what your take would be on making Tanisha an editor?"

Cassandra gave him a blank stare and tucked a loose strand of dirty blonde hair behind her ear. "She's your assistant. Do you think she's up to it?"

"She has been working on some of the articles I've not had time to review. She's done really well there, and I think she's where you were before I cut you loose and made you an editor."

"Where I was? You had me doing everything but sign your name and sometimes you had me doing that as well."

Hal laughed. "Let's not exaggerate."

"Who's exaggerating?" she asked with a smile. "I was your walking day planner, article hunter, and file gatherer.

Oh, and name an article that you got that I didn't have to examine before you signed off on it."

"All right. Perhaps, I had you doing a lot more than she is doing, but she's close," said Hal with a laugh before he held up his finger and thumb with no room between them, "I'd say about this close."

"Okay, let me stop giving you a hard time. Make her an editor," she said with a smile. "You don't need me to green light your decision, so why did you really call me in here?"

Hal crossed his arms in front of him and leaned back in his chair. He chewed on the inside of his cheek for a moment and then waved his hand around to the office. Cassandra followed the motion and took in the modern décor of less is more that Hal preferred. There was nothing new in the office that she could see. He had the same leather chairs, black metal desk, and matching bookshelf that he always had in there for as long as she could remember.

"What? There is nothing in here that's changed and it still smells like essence of Old Man so the paint's not new. What does this mean?" she asked and imitated Hal's gesture.

"Is this where you see yourself? I mean, do you want to be the editor in chief one day of this paper?"

Cassandra felt her heart sink. "You're not thinking of retiring now are you?"

"No, not yet," answered Hal.

"Then why ask me something like that? You're not sick are you?"

Hal laughed and the blush returned to his bearded cheeks. After a moment, he regained his serious demeanor and sat forward so that his elbows rested on the desk. "I ask because I want to know what your plan is for the future, Cass. You and I both know that this paper is not going to be around much longer with the way things are going. If it survives at all, we'll be on the Internet and there is no guarantee that we'll be able to compete there."

"Talk about doom and gloom. I thought that we were going to remain positive and continue to distribute to the Metro area? Where is all this coming from?"

"Between you and me?" he asked.

"Yes, of course."

"I just got off the phone with the lawyers and it seems our friends across town gave us an offer," he said. "The offer is to sell and merge, if I choose to take it."

"Do what?"

Hal raised his hands. "The Daily Herald will still exist and report as we always have on local topics, but they would be our parent company."

"Come on. You know that's not going to happen. They have their own editors, writers, and people. They don't need ours."

"Some of us would be let go of, sure. But, a lot of us would still have jobs."

Cassandra shook her head. "You're not considering this, are you?"

"Whatever I choose to do, it will be for the best of this paper. I have to think of how many jobs I can save here, Cass. No paper at all means: no jobs for any of our people," he said with a frown. "But, that is not really why

I called you in here. I want to know what your plans are for when I retire."

"Well, gee, I don't know. It isn't something that I think about in any real depth," said Cassandra. "I'll do good to think about it next week."

"If I remember correctly, you told me once that you wanted to be a journalist. That is what you went to college for and majored in. Isn't it?"

"Well, yes, but that was a long time ago."

"I seem to remember us talking about you possibly pursuing that back when you were getting ready to go on maternity leave, too," said Hal as he got up from his desk and sat on its edge. "Correct me if I'm wrong, but weren't you going to do that after you gave birth to Sean?"

"We talked about it but …."

"How old is he now?"

"Six. But, I don't see how that has anything to do with this. We just talked about me writing. Besides, a lot has happened since then."

Hal nodded. "I know. I was at the wedding. I was also the one you called when you walked in on Peter with that associate from his law firm, and I've been there for you during the separation. I just think that it may be time for you to start pursuing your dreams."

Cassandra rubbed her temples and then pulled her hair back into a pony tail. "I don't understand what all of this is about," she admitted.

"You and I both know that you don't want to be sitting in the editor in chief's seat. You are a great editor and I could help get you on at one of the publishing houses if that is what you want. But I just thought that before this paper is gone, you might want to give journalism a chance."

"I don't know what to say here."

"Say that you want to write."

"What about the articles I have to edit?"

"That's where Tanisha comes in. I figure that the least I can do is make her an editor and give her your workload. It'll also look good on her resume if she needs to find a job. Meanwhile, you can write and take Darren Merrick's column."

"Darren? But, he does all our heartwarming pieces. What is he going to do?"

"Darren is seeking employment elsewhere, effective immediately."

"What?"

"He told me if I didn't give him a raise he was taking another offer in New York."

"Again? That's like the third time he's pulled that stunt."

"Yeah, well, I couldn't give him a raise and he's taking the job," said Hal. "So, what do you say, Cassandra? Do you want to do this?"

"I will need a day or two to show Tanisha what I do and I will need to talk to my guys," she said. "But, before we get ahead of ourselves here, what exactly did you have in mind for my first piece?"

"There is a homeless shelter that I thought would make a good story. The Arms of Refuge, it used to belong to the Kaufler Estate."

"Kaufler Estate. Why does that name sound familiar?" she asked.

"We did an article on them around the time you first started. They were in that horrible accident on the Beltway with the jackknifed tanker and the Aston Martin."

Cassandra remembered the wreck. The car was a brand new 2002 Aston Martin Vanquish, made popular by *Tomb Raider* two years prior when the movie franchise first launched. The semi and car caused a pileup on the inner loop and blocked all lanes of traffic for hours after the tanker ignited. What stood out the most in Cassandra's mind was that a traffic camera caught everything and showed that another driver cut the trucker off causing the tanker to jackknife. It also showed that once the tanker came to a screeching halt, the trucker got out and attempted to pull the Kaufler's out of their vehicle but gave his own life in the effort.

"I remember that," she said. "That was an awful situation."

"That it was."

"They turned their estate into a homeless shelter?"

"I think it was a term of their will, although I'm not exactly sure," answered Hal. "However, it's been financed by an anonymous benefactor ever since. I think it would make for a good human interest piece," said Hal. "What do you say? Do you want to do it?"

"Give me a couple days to show Tanisha the ropes and let me adjust my schedule for Sean," she said. "What's the worst that can happen? If it doesn't work out I can always edit."

CHAPTER TWO

"**M**om, what is a homeless shelter?"
Cassandra placed the rinsed dish into the dishwasher and dried her hands on a towel. She turned to her son who sat at the breakfast nook with his coloring book and crayons. He stopped working on the dinosaur that he decided had to be red and yellow and stared at her with the intense brown eyes he had inherited from his father. She couldn't help but smile at him. He was so adorable when he gave his curious expression.

"A homeless shelter is a place where people, who don't have a home of their own, go," said Cassandra with a solemn tone.

"Don't they have a home? Why don't they have a home? Don't they have a mommy and daddy who have one?"

"Not always, Sweetheart," she answered as she returned to putting more dishes in the dishwasher.

"That's so sad. We have an extra room; can't they live here if they're nice?" asked Sean with all of the enthusiasm she would have expected if he were asking for a friend to spend the night.

"No, Sweetie, I'm afraid they can't. I would not feel comfortable with that, and your daddy would not approve of that, either."

"But why not?" he asked with a frown and a cross of his arms.

"It's hard to explain, Son."

"But, Dad lets people sleep at his house."

"Sean, I'm sure your father would not approve of letting just anyone sleep in his home or this one, for that matter."

Sean scrunched up his face and grunted. "He's a poop head."

"Sean O'Neal! What have I told you about calling people that?"

Sean lowered his head and pouted. "That it's not nice."

"It isn't nice. You shouldn't call anyone that, especially not your father."

"But Gwen says that poop head ain't a bad word, and Daddy calls you bad words and he don't get in trouble."

"First of all, what is the rule on using 'ain't'?" she asked, hoping that if she kept correcting him he would learn not to use it.

"I'm sorry. Is not."

"That's better," she said with a nod of approval. "Secondly, repeat what you said there at the end."

"Daddy calls you bad words and he don't get in trouble?" asked Sean with an uncertain tone.

"That would be what I was looking for," she said, and then as she made every attempt not to sound like she was nitpicking, she added, "Why shouldn't you use 'don't' there?"

"I'm sorry. Doesn't," said Sean. "He doesn't get in trouble."

"Very good, Sweetheart," praised Cassandra. "Now, as for your father and Gwen, just because they say something does not mean that they are right. Do you understand?"

"Yes."

"Good. Now, what have I told you about calling people hurtful things or bad names?"

"It is not the gently man thing to do."

"You are a gentleman, right?" she asked, and decided to let 'gently man' slide. He was, after all, only six.

"Yes."

"Okay, give me five for being a gentleman."

Sean smiled from ear to ear as he gave her a high five. It warmed her heart to see his enthusiasm and she struggled not to ask him what bad names Peter called her.

She refused to do that to her son. There was a part of her that wanted to know and wanted to ask. Yet, she felt that as a mother it would only end up hurting Sean in the long run. She did not want to be the kind of mother that pried information out of him just to get what was going on in Peter's life. If she really wanted to know, she just would ask Peter about it and hope that it did not result in an argument.

As a Christian, it went against her sense of morals to harm a child and from her own experiences she knew that bad mouthing Peter would only hurt her son. She did not want him to suffer any more than he already did from their being separated. He couldn't help that his father was unfaithful and there was no benefit in smearing Peter, either. She hoped that when Sean was old enough to know everything, he would look back and formulate his own opinion. Until then, she had to suck it up and pray that she was doing the right thing.

"Mommy, am I going with you to the homeless shelter?"

"No, Sweetie. Aunt Laney is coming to pick you up and you're going to go spend the day with her and the boys."

"Awesome! Can I take Lego Batman?"

"Yes, you may take Lego Batman, just don't forget to bring it back."

Sean abandoned the coloring book and crayons and took off through the apartment. His attention was now fixed on getting his stuff together to go to his aunt's and everything else ceased to matter. Children were amazing that way. One minute they were sad and wanted to bring in complete strangers they didn't know because they were homeless, the next minute they were chattering their way through the house about what a cool day it was going to be.

Cassandra smiled and leaned down to pour the soap into the dishwasher. Her cell phone buzzed to life as she closed the door and turned it on. She reached for the phone and saw that it was Geoffrey Jackson on the caller ID.

"Hello," she answered.

"Hey, Cass, it's Geoff. I sent you an e-mail with all of the stuff that I managed to find on that shelter you asked me for. I hope that it helps."

"Hold on, let me pull it up," she said and headed out of the kitchen into the dining room that she used as an office. "Um, hey, since you're on the phone, did you and Tanisha have a good time last night?"

"Yeah, as a matter of fact, we did. Thanks for letting me know that she was into me. I had no idea."

"Don't mention it. I am glad I could help," she said as she got to her desk.

"I'll be honest with you, when you told me she was going to be my new editor, I kind of felt off kilter," he admitted. "I have sort of had a thing for her for a while but she was seeing some other guy."

Cassandra hit the function keys to turn on her laptop's wireless and grinned. "Yeah, when I told her you were one of the ones that she would be editing, she started acting like a high school girl. I knew as soon as she started fidgeting and asking fifty million questions what time it was."

"So, we're still going to go over that stuff I do, so she doesn't think I am an idiot, right?"

Cassandra's smile grew even deeper as she logged into her e-mail account. "Things went that well, huh?"

"It went pretty well. I mean, we just got drinks since we're going to be seeing a lot more of each other and working together; but we danced and laughed and she wants to do that again some time."

"Good," she said with genuine delight while clicking on her in-box icon. "Okay, I got the e-mail. I will go over it and let you know if I need you to look into anything else. Oh, and we'll get together and go over all the grammatical stuff on Monday. Is that fine?"

"Yeah, that's great. I appreciate it. Half the time, I just type and don't even think about it. I guess I have gotten so used to doing it that way, I've forgotten how to do it right," he said, sounding embarrassed. "I know we've talked about that before... it's just that... I appreciate your being nice when you asked me to try to remember."

"No worries, Geoff. I will help you however I can. I just appreciate your looking stuff up for me," she said. "So, how about we agree to keep helping each other and maybe we'll both get to where we are trying to be. Deal?"

"Deal," he said. "Cassandra, again, thanks for being so patient with editing my articles these last few months. I know it's been nerve-racking."

"Thank you for taking constructive criticism."

Cassandra got off the cell phone after saying their good-byes and looked over the e-mail with its attachments. Not only was Geoff a great creative writer, but he was proving to be a remarkable investigator, too. He had more information on the homeless shelter than she had been able to find and she had used every search engine online.

In one of the attachments, she found that the Kaufler Estate was left to a Damien Oran Kaufler. He was listed as the son of Dr. Allen and Dr. Elizabeth Kaufler in the copy of the will that Geoff had scanned. She already knew that the doctors were the ones killed in the car accident and according to the obituary she found, they were survived by a son and Dr. Allen Kaufler's mother. However, there was no listing of the son's name in the obituary.

"Okay, so you got the estate and then what happened?" she asked the monitor.

Cassandra poured over the rest of the information that Geoff dug up. Most of it centered on the two doctors. Dr. Elizabeth Kaufler had been a promising neurosurgeon who worked at Johns Hopkins in Baltimore, Maryland.

When she had not been in surgery, she was making an hour commute back and forth from Baltimore, she thought. That made little sense to Cassandra but she wasn't a doctor; and from all the awards that the woman received it seemed that she was excellent at what she did.

There were also articles about Dr. Allen being a promising psychiatrist in Washington and how he attended many of the functions at the White House. One of the attachments had a list of all the clients he had just before the accident. Each name was blacked out in that secret service sort of fashion, which made her wonder how many politicians were seeing the doctor, but she knew that the names were blacked out due to patient-client privilege and nothing more.

Despite the amount of information contained in all that Geoff had found, there was nothing that really helped Cassandra pinpoint how the estate became a homeless shelter. Everything that she glanced over talked about either the success of the doctor's practice in the DC area, or about his son's decision to attend George Washington University in the pursuit of an anthropology degree, rather than psychology. It's a start, though. *At least I have a new lead to pursue,* she thought.

The doorbell rang heralding the arrival of her sister. She logged out of the e-mail account and got up to answer the front door. Before she could get through the adjacent living room to get to it, Sean came running down the hallway shouting Aunt Laney, Aunt Laney and hurled himself at the handle. He had the deadbolt unlocked and the door opened in the blink of an eye, but the chain prevented him from throwing it wide open, so he peered out through the crack with a massive smile.

"Hi, Aunt Laney, Mommy's got to get up there," he said as he pointed to the chain. "I can't reach."

"Back it up, Mister. Back it up," said Cassandra as she got to the door. She held up a finger to her sister through the crack, and then shut it to disengage the chain.

"Hey, kiddo," said Laney as Sean enveloped her legs with a hug no sooner than the door was open. "Do you have all your stuff together?"

"Not yet, but almost."

"Well, why don't you go get all your stuff together so you and I can go get ice cream before going to my house?"

"Ice cream?" he asked with a smile that lit up his face.

"Yeah, ice cream."

"Yay!" he shouted all the way through the apartment.

"Hi, Sis," said Cassandra while giving Laney a hug. "I appreciate you picking him up and taking him for the day."

"No sweat, I'm just glad we moved and are closer to you now."

The two sisters hugged each other and then stepped back with sincere smiles. They were much closer now than they were as kids, and Cassandra was happy about that. As the oldest, she had always been the brainy one that Laney got compared to on a regular basis and asked why she was not as smart as Cassandra. All of that changed at puberty when Laney filled out first and became the daughter that their mother could doll up and take shopping. Then it was Cassandra's turn both at school and at home, to suffer through those awkward years of physical comparison and be found lacking.

The sad part was she knew that they both were highly intelligent and they favored one another. Laney was smart; she just never cared enough to do all of her work. The more her grades were held up to Cassandra's report cards, the less she tried. The physical comparisons were a little different, though. It was not like Cassandra could help that she never blossomed into the C-cup that Laney did; but she was satisfied with the B-cup that she did get. Plus, both of them could swap jeans after children, which had come in handy when Cassandra and Peter separated and she needed to borrow clothes until she felt comfortable going back into the house.

"How do you like the new house?" Cassandra asked as they walked back toward the kitchen.

"It is going to take some getting used to but so far so good," answered Laney with a hint of apathy.

"You don't sound overly thrilled. What's wrong with it?"

"Oh, it's nothing. Besides, you'll think I'm being silly," she said with a grimace of embarrassment.

"No I won't. Out with it," said Cassandra as they sat down at the table.

"I don't like being alone there."

"That's normal. It's a new house. You're just not used to it yet."

"No, it's not that. The place freaks me out when it's just me there. I feel like I'm being watched and..." she trailed off and shook her head.

"And what? You have blinds up, right? Is there a peeping tom on the prowl out there that I need to be aware of?"

"No. It's nothing like that. I just, I hear walking and doors clicking shut..."

Cassandra was shocked. "Are you saying what I think you are?"

Laney threw her hands up. "See, that's why I didn't want to tell you."

It was hard for Cassandra not to laugh. She tried to keep a straight face because her sister's expression showed that she was serious. However, her attempt to stifle her amusement was not working very well. Anytime someone brought up the possibility of ghosts and spirits, Cassandra thought of all the scary stories and television shows that added to the hype of such phenomena. In all her years, she had never experienced a haunting and as far as she was aware the dead did not linger as apparitions according to the Bible.

Laney pointed at her and scowled. "See, that right there isn't very nice, Sis."

"I'm sorry but we're a little old to be scared of the boogeyman."

"There you go making fun of me. It's not funny, Cass. I'm serious."

"Okay, okay. I'm sorry," she said and forced herself to be serious. "It's a new place, there are bound to be sounds that you aren't used to yet. Plus, if you're anything like me, you're probably hyperaware of everything right now because it is a new place."

"That's what I keep telling myself," said Laney as she looked down the hall to see if Sean was coming. "It's getting weirder, though. Stuff I put in one place turns up in another. I ask the boys if they touched it, and they don't know what I'm talking about."

"Maybe Chris moved it, did you ask him?"

"By boys, I mean husband included."

Cassandra smiled at that and so did Laney. If ever there was a man that fit into the category of a big kid, it was Chris. For most of the people that knew him, they saw the Army-tough image he presented that had equal parts machismo and the suave, debonair crap that guys spread on thick. There was no denying that he was tough just as there was also no denying that he was a real good-looking guy; tall, muscular, with blonde hair and blue eyes. However, what made him attractive to Laney was that behind closed doors he got in the floor with their sons and played with action figures; he helped build forts and protect them against invaders; and video games did not stand a chance when the three of them were involved.

"What does Chris have to say about it?"

"He thinks I have post-buyer depression. His words not mine," she said. "And, you know he's like you, he doesn't believe in ghosts."

Cassandra shrugged. "I have heard of postpartum depression and buyer's remorse, but I have never heard of post-buyer depression. Is that even a real thing?"

"Knowing Chris, probably not," said Laney with a laugh.

Before they could continue with the conversation, Sean came into the kitchen with his book bag saying, "I'm ready, Aunt Laney! Can we get ice cream now?"

"I guess that's my cue."

Cassandra and Laney got up from the table as Sean bounced from one foot to the other. They couldn't help but smile at his impatience to get the show on the road. Cassandra knew how his one track mind worked. Nothing else mattered in the present moment except for whatever flavor of ice cream he had set his heart on while getting his things together.

"Wow, kiddo, you're not even going to miss me, are you?"

"*Mom*," he said with half a grin and half a pout, "I always miss you, but I'm getting ice cream with Aunt Laney!"

"I know, but you better be good for her and don't eat the ice cream too fast. You know you get brain freeze," said Cassandra as she walked him to the front door with Laney. She knelt down in front of him as her sister opened the door and gave him a hug. "I love you most times infinity, kiddo."

"I love you most times infinity, too."

Laney took Sean's hand and walked out the door with him, while Cassandra stood in the threshold and watched them head for the elevator. It was difficult for her to watch him leave even though she knew it would only be for a short while. A part of her already felt like she did not get to spend enough time with him since she and Peter rotated weeks. She hoped that she could write a worthy story on the homeless shelter to make sacrificing her Saturday afternoon with him worth it

"See you later, Sis," said Laney as the elevator door opened.

"Yeah, see you later and as for what we talked about earlier," replied Cassandra as she gave a telling look at Sean, "let's just keep that between us."

"Absolutely."

Cassandra waved to Sean until the elevator closed and then she stepped back into the apartment. She walked through the living room and then back into the makeshift office where she retrieved the name of the shelter's director from her desk. She folded the paper and stuffed it into her slacks' pocket and then made sure that everything was turned off.

"You've got this!" she said to her reflection in the picture over her desk.

CHAPTER THREE

The old Kaufler estate was a two-story brick mansion with immaculate hedgerows, a cobbled drive, and matching sidewalks in the heart of Georgetown. It certainly was not what one thought of when picturing a homeless shelter. The only telltale indication that it wasn't an actual residence was the wrought iron sign that hung over the entry gate, which read: "The Arms of Refuge."

Cassandra pulled into the drive and got out of the car, mesmerized by how gorgeous the house was. It was hard for her to believe anyone would turn such a breathtaking home into a homeless shelter. It didn't make sense to her. Either Damien Kaufler was a true unselfish egalitarian, or there was some sort of scheme beneath it all.

She believed that God let there be rich people in the world who had open hearts. There were men who donated all the wealth they had to the Church, others gave in secret to non-profit organizations, and there were some who were just generous and enjoyed giving to those who were less fortunate. There were also all sorts of charities and not for profit organizations that contributed to their communities and did their best to lift up those that needed it. However, Cassandra had never heard of anyone turning their family mansion into a homeless shelter.

She reviewed and edited a wide variety of articles, some of which she read with a close eye on the topic. Others she looked at from a professional perspective. In her years in the business, she knew that everyone had an opinion on what was accurate in the headlines and what was not. She did her best to stay out of those arguments because articles that did not interest her were articles she chose not to read. The articles that she read and enjoyed were the ones where people helped people in their communities and did their best to lift up their fellow man.

If she had it her way, every story that came across her desk would be one where everyone helped and loved their neighbor as themselves. However, the world was not quite there. She hoped that the Arms of Refuge turned out to be a heartwarming story. It was horrible that the Kauflers and the man driving the rig died as a result of someone's reckless driving. Yet, she hoped that God had a purpose for all of it. Her fear was that there was something far less noble going on than met the eye.

As she looked around at some of the features, the front door opened and a short dark-haired woman in her mid to late forties stepped out. She reminded Cassandra of a librarian or school teacher with her glasses and hair-do but she guessed her for a secretary or counselor, given where they were.

"Hello, how may I help you?"

"Hi, I'm Cassandra O'Neal. I'm with the Daily Herald. I called yesterday to set up an interview..."

"Oh, yes, we've been expecting you. I'm Sheryl Browning. I'm one of the house counselors. If you will, just follow me. I can take you in so our Executive Director can meet with you."

Cassandra followed the woman up the stone sidewalk and entered the house through the double front door. She was awestruck by the spacious foyer that she stepped into with its grandiose chandelier hanging from the vaulted ceiling and the marble floor that gave way to a curved stair that led up to the second floor.

Sheryl gave her a moment to take it in and then led her to the right through a set of French doors into a room that Cassandra imagined was once a formal sitting room. The only thing that gave it away as a reception area was the tall desk that said "reception" on the front; and it still maintained all the grace and elegance expected within that type of home.

Sheryl gestured to a chair for Cassandra to have a seat and said, "Give me a moment, please, while I get the director."

Cassandra gave her a warm smile and sat down as Sheryl left out another door in the back. In the room by herself, she did the only thing there to do: she gawked at everything around her. From the mahogany crown molding that lined the top of the wall, to the ornate gold wall socket plates, the Persian rug that covered the hardwood floor, and the Louis XIV chairs. It was clear that she was not in the same tax bracket as the Kauflers had been, and she knew that it had to have taken a lot of hard work to achieve what they had.

She waited for several minutes before the door in the back reopened, revealing a rather tall, very professional-looking woman. Cassandra noticed the woman's classy business attire was similar to what she herself looked for on the racks at most department stores. Her dark brown hair was pulled up in a French twist that revealed her neck and she wore minimal makeup in a plain Jane sort of fashion. Cassandra instantly envied her for that because she could never pull off the sans makeup look.

Cassandra stood up as the woman entered the room and made her way over to meet her.

"Good afternoon, you must be Director Klark, it's a pleasure to meet you," she said and shook the director's hand. "Thank you for seeing me today."

"The pleasure is all mine I assure you; and please call me Louise. I'm just so glad that you want to do a piece on all the great work that is done here at the Arms of Refuge."

Cassandra was totally taken by surprise by how the director's deep southern accent was even more over-powering in person than it had been on the telephone. She tried to not let it show, but she couldn't help but think of the movie *Steel Magnolias*.

"Well, it's not every day that a million dollar estate is turned into a homeless shelter. I'm surprised that someone hasn't written this story already."

"Actually, it's three point two million, to be exact, but not everyone puts a price on extending hospitality and help to others."

Cassandra nodded and asked, "Can I quote you on that?"

"Why, certainly," Louise replied with a smile, and then added, "but, please, why don't you let me give you the grand tour and let the Refuge speak for itself?"

"That would be great. Feel free to lead the way."

Louise began the tour by taking Cassandra out the door she entered through. It opened up into a spacious room that resembled a living room but had been remodeled and turned into a sort of office area for the staff.

"Here is where we do all of the paperwork and hold group sessions for the residents. We have group meetings four times a week and a certified instructor comes in to provide life skills training every Tuesday and Thursday."

"Life skills training?"

"Yes, we try to provide our residents with all of the tools that will assist them in achieving their goals when they transition out of the Refuge. Some of the skills that our instructor covers are things like balancing a checkbook, creating a budget plan that will ensure they don't overextend their means, and learning how to bargain shop so that they can live well within their budget."

Cassandra held up a finger and pulled her notepad and pen out of her purse. She jotted everything down that Louise just said and circled life skills instructor. She had never heard of such a thing but thought that it was a brilliant idea. Once she finished with her notes she looked back to Louise and smiled.

"I have never heard of life skills training."

"There are programs all over the nation for life skills training. When we were in school it wasn't even thought about but nowadays it's taught in elementary schools on up into high schools to at-risk youth. They also have similar classes for those who have not yet received their diplomas and are working toward getting their GEDs."

"That's good to know. My son is only in first grade. His school seems so different than when I was a kid."

Louise continued the tour and led her out of the group room into a hallway. The hall ran left and right but they went left until they came into a massive kitchen with an attached dinette. The dinette was big enough that it wouldn't have qualified as one in a normal house but Cassandra knew that that was what it was supposed to be.

"Here we have the kitchen and dining area. All the meals are prepared by the residents themselves except on major holidays. At Christmas and Thanksgiving, a caterer comes in to prepare something special for them, and we open our doors to any family or friends that they wish to invite with a limit of two guests per resident."

"Family or friends can come? What if they have more than two family members who wish to be here with them?"

"Child, if they have a family, then they are welcome to spend it with them at their home. Sometimes turning to family is not an option. Other times it's a matter of pride and wanting to succeed to show that they can make it," said Louise. "Those who have family usually have a parent, brother or sister, or their children. We make exceptions to the rule depending on how many people attend."

"How often are the functions full?"

"Every time we have one it's full. More often than not, they come in to get warm and eat, and then they ease out so that the next man or woman can enjoy some of the festivities. We coordinate with a local taxi, and several fine officers from the Metro Police volunteer in the event that anything gets too unruly."

"Has there ever been a problem before at these holiday events?"

"No. But there is always that possibility. More often than not, an outburst is due to an unaddressed mental health issue rather than greed," Louise said with a twinge of sadness.

"Oh," said Cassandra stunned. "What sort of mental health issues?"

"You'd be surprised. We have seen cases for everything from PTSD, to schizophrenia. It is one of the reasons we keep counselors on staff here 24–7," she said. "A lot of people assume that all homeless people are beggars. Some are. A lot are not. There are some who choose the lifestyle because it's what they want. We have had veterans walk through our doors, businessmen who have lost their jobs and have nowhere else to go, and women who have fled abusive relationships and ended up on the streets."

"That's horrible," said Cassandra. "How do you turn them away at the end of the evening?"

"It pains us to have to turn guests away at the end of the evening. We know that they aren't going to a warm home. However, we provide them with blankets, hygiene packages, gloves, and thick socks as gifts from the Refuge and the residents before they go; and for those that want it, we place them on our waiting list and give them the names of other shelters that the taxi can take them to."

Cassandra felt tears well up and had to pretend to be distracted by a painting on the wall. She was starting to regret not bringing Sean with her. The things that the director shared thus far were pretty moving and demonstrated the kind of generosity she wanted her son to learn and cultivate as values.

"Would you like to see some of the rooms? I have been given permission to show you the second floor."

Cassandra nodded and let the director guide her back to the front of the house and up the stairs. Paintings of influential people hung on the walls of the hall and up the stairs that she did not pick up on when she first entered the house. Martin Luther King Jr., Gandhi, Jesus, and Buddha were the first that Cassandra saw; and then came Stephen Hawking, Einstein, Aristotle and others that she was not sure about.

At the top of the stairs, Cassandra turned to Louise and asked, "May I inquire about the paintings?"

Louise smiled. "They were donated to us by Mr. Kaufler. As part of our Mission Statement, the Arms of Refuge seeks to show acceptance to all people, regardless of race, faith, sex, or age. I know it's a pretty standard statement made by a lot of organizations, but Mr. Kaufler believes strongly in co-existence. The paintings are a way of reminding all of us here that beautiful hearts and minds traverse all social lines."

"That was rather poetic. May I quote you there, as well?"

"Wish I could take the credit for it but that is what he says in each card whenever a painting is delivered."

"Is it possible for me to get in contact with Mr. Kaufler in case he would like to make a comment of his own?"

"I can e-mail him for you but there is no guarantee that he'll respond. He's a rare kind of man that avoids recognition and the spotlight. In fact, I doubt there is a single person here that can say they have ever met him in person."

"Really? You mean the staff here not just the residents?"

"Yes, I mean the staff. The residents only stay here for eight to twelve months before they transition out. I have been the director here since it opened and aside from e-mails, I have never even had the privilege to make his acquaintance."

Cassandra jotted that down in her notes. She didn't understand why Kaufler wanted to avoid being photographed or why he stayed away from the estate. Most people wanted some sort of recognition for their success and to be commended for their benevolence. Although, there were others who felt that such recognition went against their reason for being generous to begin with and they chose to keep themselves removed from such spectacles.

"So, how many rooms are available at this shelter?" asked Cassandra after she finished her notes on Mr. Kaufler.

"There were originally six bedrooms and a romp room on the second floor, after they remodeled, those rooms sleep a maximum of thirty-seven adults."

"How big are those rooms?"

"Most of the rooms are at least eight-by-nine, I guess," said Louise. "Basically, all of the bedrooms on the second floor were turned into two rooms. Depending on the size of the room, there are two to four beds per room and each bed has its own dresser and nightstand. I think that of our thirteen rooms on the second floor, all of them have at least two beds, three of them have three, and the two rooms that were made out of the romp room, both have four."

As they walked down the second floor hallway, Cassandra jotted that down and noticed that each room had its own apartment style door with a deadbolt. She touched one, saying, "I see these have deadbolts, does each of the residents has his own key?"

"Yes, each resident has his own key. This is one of the ways that we try to give our residents some privacy. We do our best to room compatible people when we can but in most of these rooms, we prefer to occupy them with families."

"So, these aren't the only rooms you have available?"

"Oh, honey, no. We prefer to think of the second floor as the family floor, the ground floor as the roommate floor, and the basement as the singles floor."

"So, you have rooms on every floor? That sounds like a lot of people. I've also noticed that I haven't seen a bathroom yet for all of these people."

"Well, right this way," said Louise with a wave of her hand.

Cassandra followed her down to the end of the hall and they entered a large bathroom area that reminded her of a cleaner, more elegant version of a college dorm bathroom. There were four sinks with vanity mirrors, three toilet stalls, and three private shower stalls as well. Even though it was a bathroom built for multiple people, it was still a beautiful room.

"There is a bathroom just like this on each floor," said Louise.

Cassandra knew that even though it was a bathroom designed for multiple residents, the tile, self-flushing toilets, automatic water spouts for the sinks and quality everything made the renovations to her own bathroom look a little bit sad in comparison. She walked over to the sink and looked at the granite countertop with longing.

"I wanted something like this in my bathroom."

Louise laughed and said, "Don't we all. I believe there was a clause in the will of the estate that specified all remodeling be done on par with the spirit of the original décor. So, although, the automatic sinks and toilets, and the single shower stalls are a new addition for sanitary purposes, the tile and the granite are the lasting legacies of the estate. Go ahead and take a look."

Cassandra proceeded to open one of the opaque glass doors to one of the stalls. Inside, the three walls were covered with the same tile that was seen in the rest of the bathroom. There were two granite shelves in the back corner to hold soaps and shampoos. The shower head was one that Cassandra had looked at during her remodel and couldn't afford. It was very nice and more upscale than she could ever afford.

She closed the stall door and turned back to Louise. "So, as a not for profit organization, how do you manage to finance all of this? You must have some serious donors to be able to accommodate your residence with all of the finer luxuries."

Louise motioned to the door of the bathroom, "Perhaps we should discuss that somewhere other than the bathroom. Does out in the conservatory with some sweet tea suit you?"

THE HAND OF REFUGE |

Cassandra agreed and they retreated through the upstairs to the first floor and then on to the conservatory. As they made their way through the mansion, Cassandra realized that she had still not seen the first homeless person and wondered where they were.

"Where are all of your residents?"

"Why, child, it's Saturday, they are in the theater room, of course."

"Theater room?"

"Oh, there is a rather large movie room in the basement adjacent to the library, single rooms and the residents' laundry. It actually has theater seating and there's a popcorn machine."

Cassandra started to think that it would almost be better to be homeless and stay at the Arms of Refuge shelter than to dish out what she did in rent each month on top of the rest of her bills. Her train of thought was further compounded by the view once she and Louise made their way into the conservatory. Just beyond the glass walls of the room, a pristine in-ground pool, replete with its own diving board and mosaic tile bottom stood between her and a pool house that she thought might have been as big as her apartment.

Louise showed her to one of the patio tables and retrieved a pitcher from the dry bar that stood against the wall, along with two glasses. After she poured them some tea she sat down and produced a pack of cigarettes. Cassandra declined her offer of one of the cigarettes but insisted she did not mind if she smoked.

"This is the only place where the residents and staff are allowed to smoke. I have tried to quit, but I tell you the truth, those electronic cigarettes just do not do the trick and the patches make me itch something terrible."

"I hated the patches, too; and the gum made my throat scratchy. It was terrible."

"How did you ever manage to quit? You must share your secret."

"Honestly, his name is Sean."

"Boyfriend?"

Cassandra shook her head. "Son. When my husband and I found out we were pregnant, I picked up a cigarette and lit it, I took a couple draws, and then it hit me: I had a life inside me. I put the cigarette out and haven't smoked since."

"You are more determined than I," she said. "I have prayed on it and asked God to let me put them down. If I can make it past the first three days, I can go for about a week and then I can't take it any longer."

"It's not easy," said Cassandra. "Gum works wonders. Some people even use toothpicks."

"I chewed a lot of gum, but toothpicks I've never tried."

"You don't ever want to quit the way my husband did."

"How did he quit?"

"He had a molar removed and was so scared of getting dry socket that he listened to the doctor and refused to smoke. Unfortunately, he forgot about a straw being the same as a cigarette and ended up getting dry socket anyway."

Louis shook her head. "That would be one way of quitting, but I think I would rather go about it an easier way. Now, you were asking me earlier..."

"I think I understand everything, feel free to interject and help me understand it better if you would."

"Sure."

"Damien Kaufler owns the estate, which I assume he uses some of his money for upkeep and so forth, right?"

"I suppose," said Louise. "I would imagine that he does."

"The Refuge is a nonprofit shelter, right? Or, is it not-for-profit?" asked Cassandra, unsure of which was which or if there was a difference in the moment.

"I get the two confused, as well. Nonprofit is what we have here. It's an organization that's not meant to make money."

"We receive a lot of our donations from former residents. Others donate out of having heard about us from former residents; and we've had and held fundraisers with the help of our local law enforcement. Yet, the major expenses, like for the remodeling and other unforeseen expenditures that come up here and there are donated by an unnamed benefactor that we all know is the Estate. Kaufler makes sure that it gets paid."

Cassandra was astonished. "The Estate pays it?"

"That's right. Whenever we need anything, the Estate pays for it."

"You said earlier that Mr. Kaufler is the owner of the Estate still. I know in my own research I could not find where he sold it. So, does that mean he not only owns the house the shelter is ran out of, but that he funds it all personally?"

"Well, the lawyers have it all set up in such a way but that is the gist of it; and I am sure that they have him covered in taxes and so forth so he gets it all back. However, the man deserves a medal for his service to this community."

Cassandra was at a loss for words. If ever there was a candidate for a saint, she thought she might have found one. "Are you sure that I can't speak to him?"

"Honey, we can send him an e-mail but beyond that, there are only two other people I know of that know how to get in touch with him."

"Can you give me their names?"

"Well, one is his lawyer, Mr. Salam. I have that number in the office although he is under instruction not to speak to anyone by Mr. Kaufler. The other is Doc, the man that Mr. Kaufler lets stay in the pool house. He is a strange duck, if you understand me, but he takes care of the Refuge's library and grounds."

"That's perfect. Is he here? I would really appreciate being able to talk to him."

Louise held up a dainty hand. "Let me forewarn you about Doc. He and Mr. Kaufler went to college together and were roommates, from what I understand. But, and this stays off the record, too... I don't want this in the papers."

Cassandra nodded.

"Doc is a very abrupt and standoffish sort of man, at least with most people. But, he has visitors that come to see him. I once walked up on him with some of his visitors and they were talking about holding a séance of some sort."

"A séance?"

"Yes, now he tried to tell me I heard wrong, that they were talking about a sendoff party for one of their other friends. But, I know what I heard and it did not sound like 'sendoff' to me. Plus, I have seen those statues of his in the pool house."

"Statues?"

"That's right, statues. Now, I know that Buddha has his own statue, which Doc has but that's not what his other statues are. So, don't be alarmed; but I believe that he might be an idolater," she said and tapped the charm dangling from her necklace before pointing at Cassandra's. "That is off of the record, of course."

Cassandra gave Louise a blank stare despite being aware that the southern belle pointed at the cross she wore around her neck. On one hand, she could appreciate Louise giving her a heads up that Doc might be into some strange stuff. On the other hand, she recognized that it was that prevalent mindset among Christians that turned people away from Jesus.

"Of course," she intoned. "But, doesn't the Refuge's Mission Statement say, 'no matter faith, age, sex, or race'?"

"It does and I am all for that. We've had Muslims, Atheists and even a Wiccan couple here, and we do our best to accommodate," said Louise as her voice grew with concern. "However, I just do not want you to be unaware of what you're walking into or what he might say."

"What might that be?"

"He doesn't believe in any one God, from what I understand. It sort of seems like he believes in all of them."

"All of them?"

Louise nodded. "He's never said that outright that I have heard; but the few times we've talked about religion, he's been rather pigheaded about it."

"Pigheaded? How so?" asked Cassandra.

"He just isn't very cordial at times, I don't think he means anything by it but he's…well, I'm sure that you'll see."

"I take it that you do not want that in the article?" asked Cassandra. "He's not out there sacrificing goats or calves is he?"

"I certainly hope not. I have never seen anything like that. All I am saying is that he has his own perspectives that in no way reflect the Refuge. Just like my belief in Christ does not reflect the Refuge, it is my personal belief."

"I think that I understand," said Cassandra. "Mrs. Klark, I'll be upfront with you, this is my first article and whatever someone believes here, whether staff or resident, it's not about any of you specifically, it's about the Refuge and the stories of how this place is helping others. I am not going to write an article that tears down something that's helping people because one person may or may not believe in my God; or because one person may be rude."

"Good," said Louise. "We appreciate that."

CHAPTER FOUR

W hen the conversation in the conservatory came to an end, Cassandra let Louise show her to the theater room before they set out to speak with Doc. They made their way back through the house and down the long hall that passed by the kitchen and office, and then came to a "T" in the passage where carpeted stairs descended into the well-lit basement.

Cassandra could hear the sounds of a movie playing before the theater came into view. Had she not known that she was in someone's house, she would have believed that she was stepping down into an area of one of the local cinemas, albeit back in the 50s. What she expected for a popcorn machine turned out to be one of the older kinds on wheels. It put a smile on her face and made her mouth water as the smell of the butter hit her.

"As you can see, ahead of us is the theater; to the right over there is the laundry and the bath area for this floor, and down that hall," she said pointing to the left, "that leads to where our single men and women reside."

"Living quarters and the theater are the only rooms?"

"No, there is also a library behind these stairs that runs along the back. I guess it's the back left of the house? You go in through this door here," she said and walked to the door and opened it.

Cassandra looked in and saw a younger looking woman examining the books that stood on one of the shelves and there was a guy in his mid-twenties that sat in the floor of the aisle reading as she'd seen done in almost every bookstore she went into.

"Are your books up to date?"

"Some are, others are timeless classics," said Cassandra. "A lot of these books are from the great grandfather and grandfather Kaufler, while others are from the Kauflers before they passed away. The newer books come from what Doc is allotted to put into it."

"The grandfather and great grandfather?" asked Cassandra.

"Yes, great grandfather Dedrick Kaufler ran a bookstore for years that started out as a bookbinding and repair shop for collectibles. It changed when the grandfather, Wilbert, took over and eventually what was left of the books came here when Wilbert passed away."

"What can I expect to find in there?"

"A little bit of everything. There are scholarly, religious, and academic works that the doctor owned. There are classics and fiction. There's an assortment of romance novels courtesy of Mrs. Dr. Kaufler, I presume; and there are children and young adult books from when Mr. Kaufler was in school. That isn't including what Doc puts on the shelves."

"Everyone here can check them out and read them?"

Louise nodded. "We have one rule: bring back whatever you leave out of here with. Most everyone follows that rule. We've had a few books go missing but nothing substantial enough to lock the library up."

Cassandra stepped back out of the doorway and pointed across the hall as laughter erupted inside the theater. She really wanted to get a chance to see the residents as they watched a movie. Louise smiled and gave her a polite nod before she led the way across the hall.

In the theater room, she found the residents enjoying a drama that she recognized and she was pleased to see that Louise had not exaggerated one bit about the seating or the popcorn machine. The movie was coming to its climatic end as they took a seat in the back and afterward she got the opportunity to interview two of the Refuge's residents.

The first person that she talked with was an older gentleman named Oscar who lost his home to a bank foreclosure after losing his job when the economy tanked. The second was a mother of two named Julie who lived on the second floor with both of her daughters. Julie's husband was an abusive alcoholic, who beat her and her daughters until she decided that being homeless had to be better than suffering his abuse.

Both stories tugged at Cassandra's heartstrings and made her eyes well up. She could remember times when she gave money to the homeless she passed in her car and Peter would berate her for it.

He had always maintained that they could get jobs and do what every other American did to earn their own way, and Cassandra knew there were times she had bought into his crap. What she discovered as she talked to Julie and Oscar was a very different reality than the stereotypes that so many believed were accurate.

She walked away from the interviews with them and found that she needed a moment alone. She asked Louise where the bathroom was on the basement level and then excused herself to head there. All she wanted to do was shut herself up in a stall so that she could collect herself.

She put toilet lid down and sat on the toilet. The tears flowed from her eyes and she felt humbled and ashamed. There was so much in her life that she took for granted. She had a stable career that provided for her and Sean. She had a nice apartment that she and her son could come home to; and she had a reliable car that got them where they needed to be.

Sure, Hal could sell The Daily Herald and merge it with The Washington Post, but she would still be able to find work if they chose to let her go. Sure, the apartment was not the beautiful split level house that she and Peter bought and then chose to sell two years later when they separated but it was home. She had so much to be thankful for and felt horrible that it took coming to a homeless shelter to realize how blessed she was.

She wiped the tears that cascaded from her eyes and then retrieved her cell phone from her purse. In her contacts, she selected Hal and sent him a text message.

Cassandra typed: *Just want u 2 know, at shelter. Don't know how Merrick could keep askin 4 raises doing i.views like this. Guess I'm a sissy.*

After a few minutes, Cassandra's cell phone buzzed and showed a new text message. She clicked on it and saw that Hal responded with:

Not true. You feel. He did not. That's what'll make u great at it.

Cassandra smiled. She sent a quick thank you back and told him that she had to get back to it before she stuffed the phone in her purse. Outside of the stall she was glad that there was nobody else around since she looked like a raccoon from where her mascara streaked down her cheeks. She fixed it in the mirror and hoped that it wouldn't be too noticeable before she set out to find Louise.

The director stood just outside of the theater room waiting on her as she exuded that whited sepulcher southern charm. Cassandra wanted to like the woman but after the way she said idolater, it was hard not to see her as a hypocrite. She knew she was no better for judging Louise and chastised herself for it.

"Everything all right?" asked Louise.

"Everything's fine. I think I have almost everything I need. The last thing that I would like to do is speak with Doc and see if he can get me in contact with Mr. Kaufler."

"Ms. Browning went out to check with him while you interviewed Julie and Oscar, he said that he will speak with you out by the pool house patio," said Louise. "I apologize for not accompanying you but there are some other matters that I must now attend to. When you are finished, Ms. Browning will show you out. Is that okay?"

"That is fine." Cassandra looked around for Sheryl Browning but did not see her anywhere. "Is Ms. Browning going to walk me out to the pool house...?"

"I thought that you might like to take a stroll by yourself, that way you can get a feel for the place without us hovering. But, if you would like for her to..."

"No, no. That is fine. That's a rather good idea, actually," said Cassandra. "Thank you, Ms. Klark. This has been a profound experience."

"Well, that is wonderful to hear. I hope it inspires a profound article," replied Louise. "It was a pleasure to meet you."

"Thank you for having me."

Cassandra watched the director head back into the theater and was glad that she had the walk to the pool house alone. She made her way to the stairs and thought about what Julie and Oscar had to say about the Refuge.

She wanted to fit their stories into the article along with the praises that they gave to the shelter, but she was not quite sure how she would do it yet. Before she talked with them, her plan was to focus on the philanthropy efforts of Damien Kaufler in Capitol Hill's backyard but after hearing their stories, her idea had transformed.

When she arrived at the pool house, she thought that she had a solid plan for how to write her article. She wasn't even sure if she needed to talk to Doc anymore but he had agreed to speak with her and she was already there. She figured that she would make it quick and if he had anything that she could incorporate into the article, then that would be great.

As she approached, Doc sat with his back to her at the pool house's patio table and typed away at a laptop. From the back, all she could make out was that he had dark hair that was sort of long on top but clean cut, and jeans and T-shirt taste.

When her heel clicks on the white stonework drew closer to him, he turned to look at her and revealed a rather striking face that had the most penetrating eyes she had ever looked into. Ice blue in the way that a huskie or malamute's eyes were, Doc's eyes had an intensity to them that made Cassandra feel like he was staring right through her.

Gripped in the strangeness of his gaze, Cassandra almost failed to see why his face seemed so striking to her in that initial moment. It was not until she diverted her eyes that it dawned on her who he looked like. She tried to bring order to her thoughts as he laid the laptop down on the table and stood up, but her mind was in a chaotic spiral.

"You must be Cassandra O'Neal," he said and extended his hand.

She took it and tried not to be weird. "I am. You must be Doc."

Doc smiled and scratched his head. "You have a bit of blushing going on there; do I have something in my teeth?"

Cassandra put a hand to her face in an attempt to cover the blush but she knew it was no use. "I am sorry. I just... well, I couldn't help but think that you look a lot like Johnny Depp. John Dillinger, Johnny Depp, not creepy Sweeny Todd, Johnny Depp."

Doc smiled. "So, your first impression is that I am a public enemy?"

"No, just that you have that look, I mean..."

Doc raised his hands and grinned. "I know what you mean. I've heard it a lot, actually," he said. "I think that I look nothing like the man, although I appreciate the compliment."

Cassandra took the seat that he got up and pulled out for her. She hoped that she could get passed sounding like a complete fool for saying that he looked like the actor. Now that she got a good look at him, he could have resembled a lot of men that had dark hair and were clean-cut. She waited for him to close the laptop and place it off to the side and then gave him a polite smile as he sat back down at the table.

"As I am sure you know I'm here on behalf of the Daily Herald doing a piece on the shelter. I was hoping that you could help me get in contact with Mr. Kaufler for a quote or perhaps shed some light on him personally."

"I am afraid that it will not be easy to get in touch with Damien. He is currently living off the grid with minimal contact to the outside world."

"Can you at least tell me where, so that I can mention it when I explain he was unreachable for comment?"

"Only Damien truly knows where he is. Last that was heard, he was researching the shamanic practices of the Xhosa in South Africa, with plans to head to Mali afterward."

"South Africa? Well then, what can you tell me about him, if you don't mind?"

"I don't know what you want to hear, really."

"Anything that comes to mind."

"Okay. In that case, Damien is a recluse. He loathes the spotlight and prefers anonymity over being recognized. He's rich but likes to live comfortably while using his money to help others. He's a well font of information, which he's talked about putting into books. However, for all his intelligence, he is a horrible writer."

Cassandra jotted down what Doc said and then asked, "May I quote you on the being rich part?"

"Sure."

"I never caught your last name."

"McGee," he said with a smile.

"Doc McGee?"

"The one and only, even if I do look like a public enemy," he said with a smile. "Actually it's James McGee Jr. Doc is a nickname."

Cassandra blushed once again and forgot what she wanted to ask next. She glanced over her notes and decided that her plan to focus on the stories of the residents and touch on Mr. Kaufler was the way to go. Doc was not much of a help even if he was nice to look at, but she believed that her instincts told her what to write after she left the theater.

"Well, I think that about does it," she said confident she had what she needed.

"Good luck, then. I look forward to reading about it in the paper."

"You read the Daily Herald?" she asked.

"Oh, yeah. My Dad read it religiously every morning when I was a kid. He used to tell me that if I didn't shape up and fly right, he was going to make me deliver papers like the kid that delivered on our street. I guess you could say I read it because of him."

CHAPTER FIVE

THE DAILY HERALD

C assandra sipped her coffee and read through the first draft of her article. The entire story focused on the lives of the people that were enriched by the Arms of Refuge. From men and women who had been there and gone on to achieve so much once they had been given the chance to get on their feet, to those who were there and had received a renewed sense of hope that they too could regain control over their lives.

She was pleased with how she incorporated Julie and Oscars stories into it which led into the hope that they both shared for a better tomorrow based on the Refuge's dedication to their residents. Her favorite line, though, was her ending.

> *In a sanctuary that protects against the ignominy with which society regards those who have endured unimaginable loss, it becomes clear that the true discomfiture belongs to those of us who cannot bring ourselves to bear a single discomfort to assist our fellow man.*

She felt that she could not have ended it any better. Her only concern was the use of ignominy and discomfiture. It read great but she worried that it was too much. She deleted the words and typed embarrassment and disgrace in place of ignominy and embarrassed awkwardness in place of discomfiture.

With the revision in place, she re-read the line.

In a sanctuary that protects against the embarrassment and disgrace with which society regards those who have endured unimaginable loss, it becomes clear that the true embarrassed awkwardness belongs to those of us who cannot bring ourselves to bear a single discomfort to assist our fellow man.

"Well, that could work but you have to go," she said as she deleted embarrassed awkwardness, "And discomfiture will just have to be understood in context."

"Who are you talking to?" asked Hal from her office door.

Cassandra jumped a little at the unexpected sound of his voice and did her best to balance her cup through the air so she did not spill it. With the skilled success that she owed to being the mother of a five-year-old, she avoided the near disaster and set the mug down on the desk.

She scrunched her face at Hal. "You almost made me spill my coffee!"

"Sorry," he said as he raised his hands. "I didn't mean to startle you."

"No worries. I'm not wearing it, so all is good in the world."

"So, what's the computer screen saying this morning?"

"If you must know, the computer screen says I'm awesome!"

"Is that so? Well, I hope that's because you have Tanisha caught up on all that she needs to do and your article is almost finished."

"Tanisha didn't need me to catch her up on anything. She already has her ducks in a row," she said.

"Nice," said Hal.

"For me, I'm done with my first draft. All I have left is some fact checking to go over and then I'll be turning it in once I'm done."

"Good, can I expect it on my desk this afternoon?"

Cassandra nodded. "Yep."

"Excellent, well, then I will leave you to it," said Hal before he turned to leave. "Oh, one last thing…"

"Yes?"

"You know I fully expected you to start on the story today, right? You didn't have to go out there for the interview over the weekend."

"I know but I wanted to get a jump on it."

"Well, that's fine; it's just that the last time we talked I assumed that you were going to take a couple days before you did. Next thing I know, you're out there at the shelter doing an interview and everyone knows it but me."

"Are your feathers ruffled because you were the last to know?"

"Little bit. I thought we were better than that. But, as it turns out, apparently Geoff went to your son's christening and sent you to the right divorce lawyer, not me."

"I'm sorry. I will keep you better informed! And that was a divorce lawyer we still have not used!" she said as Max came up to the door behind Hal.

"Pardon me, Mr. Birchen," he said as she held up a manila folder. "I have that information for you, Mrs. O'Neal."

Hal moved aside to let the man through.

"This is everything that I could find for your fact checking," he said as he made his way across the room and handed the folder over.

Cassandra noticed that the compiled file wasn't very big but she was sure that there had to be more on Kaufler than in what Geoff had provided. His search focused on the Kaufler Estate, Dr. Kaufler, and Mrs. Kaufler, with very little said about the man she was most interested in.

"Good," said Cassandra. "Would you like to give me a rundown?"

Max looked over his shoulder at Hal and then turned his attention back to Cassandra with a grateful smile. "Damien graduated from Washington University with a Masters in Anthropology. He was near the top of his class and all of his professors believed he would go on to get a PhD. However, clauses in his parents' will stated that he had to get his Masters before he could get any of the inheritance. Once he got the Masters, he never pursued academics again.

"There are two different camps of thought as to why he never pursued his doctorate. The first camp, namely his grandmother, and a handful of his professors, believed that it was because of the money he inherited. The other camp claims that during his last year of study abroad he had a life-altering experience that caused him to become a recluse. I couldn't verify if that was the grandmother's opinion, but the family friend I spoke with swore to it;

and I couldn't verify the classmates' claim, either; so it doesn't help much in the way of facts. Sorry."

Cassandra held Max with her hazel eyes and offered an understanding nod of her head. "Anything else?"

"Nothing much aside from some childhood stuff and a single photo I managed to find from his parents funeral. I took the liberty of cropping it and enlarging it."

"Did the grandmother decline to speak with us?" asked Hal.

"Unfortunately, no," said Cassandra. "She passed away about a year ago."

"We tried to find other relatives to comment, too, but we did not have much luck," added Max.

Hal's brow furrowed. "None?"

"Kaufler is fourth generation," said Cassandra as she shook her head. "His great grandparents fled Germany to avoid the concentration camps."

"I see," said Hal.

Cassandra opened the file. "What stuff from childhood? And, this picture's fuzzy. I thought you said you enlarged it?"

Max stepped forward and looked at the picture. "I'm sorry, that was the one that I messed up. I apologize for putting it in there. Try the next one," he said, and then added, "Not a lot on his childhood, just that he grew up here in DC on …"

"No way!" exclaimed Cassandra as she smacked her desk.

"James McGee Jr. Street."

CHAPTER SIX

Cassandra never felt so livid in her life. It would have been fine if Doc declined to talk to her, then she would have never known that he and Damien Kaufler were one and the same. He had not declined, though. He had agreed to talk to her and then he lied to her face. On top of that, he had thrown every clue he could at her as to his true identity. *He had to know I would find out, he just had to.*

She pulled into The Arms of Refuge as her phone went off for the hundredth time. She did not have to look at it to know that it was Hal. He had been worried about her as she stormed out of the office and she could not blame him. If she had been in his shoes, she would have been worried about her, too.

As she threw the car into park, she knew she should tell him what was going on but she was not even sure how to explain it to him. *What do I even say? I got duped by the guy? It's my first story and I was bamboozled by a handsome face? That was not about to happen.* She had to confront Damien before she could tell Hal the whole story.

She turned the phone off and slipped it into her purse before she got out of the car. Her heels did not so much click across the white paving stones as they clanked but she did not care. There was one thing in this world that she disliked more than being lied to or cheated on and that was being made to look foolish at her job.

The double doors opened to the mansion after her third prolonged ring of the bell. A middle-aged man that she had not seen during her previous visit greeted her in a bewildered fashion. She could tell that he did not know what to do with her unexpected arrival and she took full of advantage of that fact.

"Hi, I'm Cassandra O'Neal, with the Daily Herald. I was here on Saturday and interviewed some of your staff and residents. I need to see Doc, I believe you call him. I'm sure he's expecting me."

"Um, please come in, I can see if Mr. Doc is available."

Cassandra stepped in and continued past the man. "Oh, I know where to find him. Pool house, right?"

"Ms. O'Neal, I have to … Ms. O'Neal …."

Cassandra turned back to the man and smiled. "Oh, I am sure that he knows I am coming, it will be fine. I can show myself out there."

She never gave the man a chance to catch up with her as he closed the door and if he thought for a second that she was going to stop and wait for him, he was out of his mind. She heard him make a mad dash for the reception room that she had been shown into on Saturday. Once the door slammed behind him, she took off in a half run and hoped that she could get to the pool house before Kaufler was forewarned that she was on her way.

As she made her way to the kitchens and then into the conservatory, she passed several faces that she recognized from the Refuge's theater. The residents that were out in the smoke area gave her surprised looks as she zipped through with an awkward smile and wave, but she was committed to her confrontation with Kaufler and couldn't stop to chitchat.

There was no sign of Damien waiting for her on the patio of the pool house as she expected. She was not sure if that meant he had not gotten the call yet or if he was still on the phone with the guy from the front door.

Please, don't be calling the cops. Please, don't be calling the cops, she prayed.

The French door that led into the pool house was closed she noted. She hoped that did not mean he was out. If she had stormed in to confront him and he was not there, then that would have been awful. She could see the headline in her head. Editor goes off the deep end at Refuge.

On the patio, she could hear Kaufler's voice inside and felt her heart quicken. She couldn't make out the conversation, but she figured that he was on the phone since she could not hear a second voice. She hoped that it wasn't the guy from the front door; but then again, she didn't care who he talked to, all that mattered was that he was there.

Cassandra stepped up to the closed door and knocked on it.

She heard Kaufler excuse himself in the conversation and then heard the sound of his footfalls as he headed toward her. It took all her willpower to not look inside as he neared, but she managed to keep her attention fixed on the patio until he opened the door.

"Ms. O'Neal, I had a feeling you'd be back."

"Let me just say I do not like being made a fool of...."

Kaufler raised his hands.

"I apologize for not being up front with you before but...."

"No, I'm talking here, you're listening...." she said.

"I had to be discreet because you didn't know when you sat down."

"That doesn't excuse you."

"I'm sorry. I didn't wish to lie to you," said Kaufler, as he glanced around and raised his hands. "I didn't think that you'd become this irate, either."

"You haven't seen irate. How dare you make me look like a fool in front of everyone here!"

Doc shook his head. "You don't understand, they don't know," he said in a hushed voice as he stared at the conservatory. "Or, they didn't until you showed up here like this."

Cassandra looked back at the mansion and then back at Kaufler. "What do you mean they don't know?"

"To everyone here, I'm just Doc," he said. "The director doesn't even know I'm me. Although, it won't take long for her to find out now."

"Oh my gosh, I am so sorry," she said. "I thought they all knew. Wait, why am I apologizing? Who keeps their identity hidden and then gives clues to a journalist like that? How was I supposed to know they didn't know?"

"I assumed that you would call, not show up unannounced," he said. "And, perhaps I didn't plan for your reaction to be what it was. I don't know."

Cassandra stood there for a moment and looked around in a daze. She had not felt this confused in as long as she could remember. All the angry wind in her sails was gone. Now she was just frustrated. He had let her in on the big secret of who he was while the rest of the world believed he was a world away and she had let her emotions cloud her judgment. No, this is not my fault. This is his fault for playing a stupid secret identity game. This wasn't a television show on prime time and he could have handled it a lot different.

"I have to go. I can't believe that I even came out here for this," she said and turned to leave.

"Wait, aren't you interested in why I suggested this story to your editor-in-chief?" he asked. "Aren't you curious as to why I wanted *you* to do it?"

Cassandra stopped in her tracks. She knew she heard him wrong. Hal never mentioned that she was requested specifically for this article. He pitched it as her way to get into what she had always wanted to do.

She turned around and glowered at Kaufler. "You expect me to believe that?"

"Call and ask him yourself."

Cassandra did not hesitate to do just that. She reached in her purse and pulled out her phone. After she turned it on, she clicked on one of the missed calls from Hal and pressed the green phone button. Kaufler leaned back against the pool house while she held the phone up to her ear. On the second ring Hal answered.

"Cassandra, are you all right? You left here in a fit."

"Oh, I've been better, Hal. Remember that little guilt trip you laid on me earlier about being the last to know?

Tell me something, was I requested specifically for the Refuge story?"

Silence fell on the other end of the line.

"Hal?"

"Nobody has ever been allowed inside to cover the story, Cassandra. I was going to …."

"So, let me get this straight. You knew that I was asked for specifically and you failed to clue me in?" she asked as she walked away from the pool house to get a little more privacy.

"Yes, I knew," he admitted. "Mr. Kaufler asked for you and told me that he wanted to see how the piece went and if it went well he wanted to see about getting you to help write and edit his memoirs. I thought it'd be a good opportunity for you, especially after the offer we got to sell and merge."

Cassandra did not know how to respond to that. She felt foolish all over again. Hal was trying to look out for her and she had dropped the ball. It had been years since she smoked a cigarette but she found herself wanting one right then.

"Damn, Hal. I wish you would have told me."

"I didn't know you were going to throw yourself into the middle of it as quickly as you did. I figured I would have time to talk to you about it some more."

"Well, I threw myself into it, all right," she said as she glanced over her shoulder. "Pray that I come out smelling like a rose. I have to go."

"Good luck."

Cassandra hung the phone up and stared at the pool while she tried to reel it all back in. *Okay, you can fix this. It's not that big of a deal,* she told herself.

She turned around and walked back to Kaufler. "Okay, so, I look like an idiot."

"No, you don't. I should have thought this through a little bit better."

"Well, I can honestly say that I've never been in a situation like this before. I'm not sure what we're supposed to do."

"Let's start over," he said and extended his hand. "I am Doc to almost everyone that knows me."

"I'm Cassandra, pleasure to meet you."

They shook hands and then started to laugh at how absurd it all was.

"I'm sure that your boss will explain why I asked for you if he didn't allude to it already while you were on the phone...."

"He mentioned something about it."

Kaufler nodded. "I am about to meet with some people here in half an hour but if you want to come in, we can discuss things more inside."

Cassandra shot a glance back at the conservatory. She was pretty sure that none of the residents had overheard the confrontation since the pool house was a good distance away. She also did not think that she ever called Kaufler by anything other than Doc to the man at the front door.

"Do you think they could hear us?" she asked.

Kaufler shook his head. "I doubt it."

"If it's any comfort I am pretty sure that I referred to you as Doc with the guy at the front door."

"How sure are you about that?"

"95% sure," she said and gestured toward the pool house door. "How much can you explain to me about this story before your guests show up?"

—ܢܢܐ—

When Damien Kaufler showed Cassandra into the pool house, she did not know what to expect beyond the French door. Louise's description of idol statues was still fresh in her mind and her imagination ran wild with images of strange altars and golden calves like the Bible mentioned.

However, that was not what she found.

She walked through the door into a large open room with a vaulted ceiling and saw that the open floor plan gave her a view of the kitchenette and what served as a living room and study. The décor of the place had a definite bachelor feel to it and was made up of a hodgepodge of stuff, but she did not see what Louise was talking about. She noticed that there was one closed door that led out of the study area but she figured it was Damien's bedroom or the pool house bathroom. *Then again*, she thought, *it could be where he keeps his statues.*

Damien invited her to take a seat on the couch and then offered her something to drink as she sat down. She accepted a bottle of green tea and gave a closer look around at the things he had on the walls and on the book shelves. The most interesting thing that she saw on the walls was a massive copy of Leonardo da Vinci's *Vitruvian Man*. On the bookshelves, there were all sorts of ornamental knickknacks and pieces of art that she guessed Louise could have mistaken for idols. But, none of it made the impression on her that the director made it sound like.

"You have a lot of interesting art," she said as Damien took a seat in one of the two Rockford style armchairs opposite the couch.

He glanced around. "I have a habit of bringing home religious iconography that inspires me."

"Like that Buddha? What is it made out of?" Cassandra glanced around at the rest of the statuettes that were on display.

"Yes. It's made out of clay. I like the principals of Buddhism, even though I sometimes find it very difficult to sit and meditate," said Doc. "Clearing the mind and trying to keep it clear is not easy."

"It requires a lot of discipline. What is their path? Right thought, right mindfulness and right action ... I don't remember the others," said Cassandra.

"Right speech, right concentration, and right understanding, I think, are in there ... that's six, right?"

"Yes, aren't there two more? I mean, it's the Eightfold Path, right?"

"Yeah, I'd have to look it up to remember," said Doc.

"Right livelihood and right effort!" exclaimed Cassandra after a moment. "I can't believe I still remember that!"

Doc laughed. "I haven't thought about the Eightfold Path in quite a while. It is amazing how the memory lets things fade."

"Have you ever practiced Buddhism?"

"I have meditated and tried to quiet my mind, if that is what you mean. As far as adhering to the principles ... I tend to look at belief systems to find out what is there that's similar. What about yourself?"

"I read up on Buddhism and some other beliefs in college just to understand what they believed. I also took a course or two on religion. Some of it was interesting," said Cassandra. "All I really remember is how karma reminded me of what God said in Galatians 6:7, about reaping what you sow."

Doc nodded. "That is a good comparison. Are you a Christian?"

"Yes. It's been a while since I have been to Church but there is only one true God in my life," said Cassandra. "What about you? Do you have a specific belief? I don't usually ask, yet I can't help but see that you have an assortment of interesting knickknacks," she said and took a sip of her tea before she sat it down on a coaster next to a wood carving of what she realized was Thor.

"It is difficult to explain my belief," said Doc. "The Infinite is beyond anything we can know and yet, God, if you like, is all around us."

"God, if I like?" asked Cassandra.

"Different people call God by different names."

"There is only one God, Mr. Kaufler."

"I am not denying that, yet I'm not exactly promoting that, either. I believe that God is as diverse as the world we live in."

"I would have to disagree. God is God and we are all diverse as his children, but he is still God."

"You are entitled to your opinion and belief," said Doc. "I am not trying to debate it with you I'm just merely stating that there are a lot more similarities among faiths than we tend to want to believe."

"So, this book?"

"I guess I have hit a nerve?"

"I believe what I believe and you believe what you believe. As long as we can respect that, then you won't offend me," she said. "Now, about this book you mentioned?"

"Actually, it's more like books," he answered. "I want to compile all that I have learned and experienced both in academics as well as outside of the classroom, into a sort of chronicle, if you will."

"Are we talking a scholarly work, a memoir or what?"

"A little bit of both, I think, mixed with descriptions of your own accounts of what you witness while assisting me."

"Assist you?"

"Perhaps 'assist' is not the right word. I will need you to assist me with writing the books, of course. But, I am hoping that you will also accompany me so that you can see for yourself what I want to write about."

Cassandra considered his words. "What sort of thing will I be seeing?"

"If I told you, you would laugh and take me as a joke."

"Okay. Try to help me understand what I will be helping you with because you are being rather vague and I prefer to know what I'm getting into."

"You believe in God. Do you believe in spirits?"

"Like ghosts?"

"Yes, ghosts, entities or spirits; some of us might call it the paranormal, while others might be more comfortable with supernatural beings or even poltergeists. The words are all synonymous, I think."

"I don't know that I believe in ghosts, Mr. Kaufler."

"You don't know or you do not believe?"

"I don't believe in ghosts. Unless, of course, the ghost is the Holy Ghost."

"Then it would be great to have you accompany me, to give your account of what you experience."

"Are you saying that you see ghosts?"

"No. I do not see ghosts."

"Do you conjure them up, then? You know with a Ouija board or a séance?"

Doc shook his head. "From my experience and studies, playing around with the other side can be dangerous. I do not believe anything can harm us unless we give it the power to harm us but at the same time, there are certain things I don't want under my roof."

"We agree on that, then," said Cassandra with a laugh. "May I ask a question that is gnawing at me?"

"Sure, ask me anything."

"Why did you ask for me? I have never written a book or a column even, all I have ever done is editorial work."

"I am not sure how to explain that right now without you running for the door."

Cassandra smiled in an attempt to hide her sudden nervousness. "Try me."

"Have you ever had a dream that you woke up from and it seemed so real and so significant that you had to ask yourself what it meant?"

"I guess," she answered.

"Have you ever dreamt about something that you should not know or that hadn't happened and then it did?"

Cassandra froze in her seat. Has he been talking to Peter? That did not make much sense, though. Damien

Kaufler had no reason to talk to Peter unless he represented him as a lawyer. There was no reason for Peter as a corporate lawyer to represent him.

"Have you ever dreamt about something and then had it happen?" he asked. "That probably sounds crazy, but there are case studies that show it has happened. Some call it being psychic or prophetic, I know. There are others that think it may just be a person tapping into a part of the collective unconscious that shows us the likelihood of an upcoming event that our psyche is trying to prepare us for."

"Like a parent dying?" she asked and immediately regretted it.

"Yeah, that could be an example. Although, our minds process all sorts of information that we are not even aware of and if that parent were around us all the time, such a dream could be the product of unconsciously picking up on an existing health condition that they aren't talking about. Unless, of course, that parent died from something unrelated to his or her health."

She was relieved that Kaufler did not flinch at the mention of a deceased parent. He was the last person on her mind when the words spilled from her lips and she was not even thinking about how his parents died. The parent she thought of was her father. She had not spoken to him in years when she dreamt that she was at his funeral one night and it bothered her so much that she confided in Peter about how she saw him in the casket in her dream.

Peter chalked the dream up to the old wives tale that his mother and grandmother believed in that dreams about someone dying meant that the dreamer was pregnant. The next day, after two pregnancy tests said that she was not with child, the phone call came. Neither she nor Peter knew what to say.

"So, I take it that you believe that the other sorts of dreams are possible. The ones where you dream of something you shouldn't know."

Kaufler nodded. "I have had a few experiences that would suggest that they do. Your being here being one of them."

"You dreamt about me helping you write your books?"

"Well, I had a group of dreams that sent me in your direction. Your name was never given but I saw you and I saw the newspapers that my father used to read. I just followed the clues."

Cassandra chewed on the inside of her lip as she let his words sink in. "This isn't some sort of prank or practical joke, is it? I mean, there isn't some guy hiding with a video camera behind that door filming all of this to make me look like an idiot is there?"

Kaufler arched his brow. "No, it isn't a prank or a joke and there's nobody filming or taping this in any way. In fact, I'd be willing to sign a contract that would entitle you to a large sum of money if it were a prank, just to ease your mind."

"To me, all of this just isn't normal. So, if I seem hesitant or reluctant, you have to understand that it's not every day that a reclusive multi-million dollar philanthropist follows his dreams to get the aid of an editor to write a series of books while going about it as you have."

"I understand. I know that all of this is rather odd," he said with a smirk. "Considering that, I have a proposal that I think you'll find agreeable."

"I'm all ears."

"Shadow me for a week. All you have to do is watch, listen and take notes. I will match your pay at the Daily Herald for that week and after that, you can make a decision on whether or not you want to work with me."

"So you'll pay me what I make at the paper for a week to shadow you?"

"Yes. And if you choose to take my offer, then we'll consider it a deciding bonus."

Cassandra thought about that and then asked for a pen and paper. Kaufler retrieved a pad from his desk and a quill pen that had a ballpoint tip and extended them out to her. She took them both and calculated her gross income for every two weeks and then wrote down the amount that she made in a week before handing it back to Kaufler.

"Two-thousand, eight-hundred, and forty-seven dollars and fifty eight cents?"

"That's right."

"Let's make it an even twenty-nine hundred."

"No, the amount on the paper is fine," she said.

Kaufler laughed. "Whatever suits you."

"If I choose to take this job, then what are we talking about pay-wise?"

"A little above the average for a non-credited ghost-writer, plus expenses."

"How much is that, exactly?"

"Eighty bucks an hour."

Cassandra felt her heart jump up into her throat. Eighty dollars an hour was a lot of money. *Eight times eight is sixty-four,* she thought; *add a zero on the end of that and that is six hundred and forty in a day!* She was not sure what that was in a week without a calculator but she knew that six times six was thirty-six and with two more zeros added to that, with whatever the leftover was, she would be looking at more than four grand a week.

"How many books are we talking here?"

Kaufler smiled but before he could answer her, the telephone on the kitchen wall rang. He held a finger up to her and got up to answer it. Cassandra pinched herself as he headed into the kitchen to make sure she was not in a dream. The pinch hurt but she had never enjoyed pain so much in her life. There was a lot that she could do for Sean and herself with that kind of money. She knew that she would have to sit down and figure it all out but if she could make twelve grand in a month's time, it was worth it.

"That was Dave at the front," said Kaufler as he hung up the phone and walked back to the armchair. "My guests have arrived."

Cassandra made to get up and Kaufler motioned for her to sit back down.

"But, your guests...."

"You might as well get an idea of what you're getting into," he said. "And all of this is off the record, so no article on what you hear today. Okay?"

"Sure," she said. "Just let me text my boss real quick to let him know I'm still here tying up some loose ends."

"That's fine. Hey, come to think of it, would you mind sitting in this chair over here and letting my guests sit on the couch? That'd probably work out a lot better."

CHAPTER SEVEN

"**D**oc, this is Samantha Pratt."
Damien Kaufler released the older man's hand
that he welcomed into the pool house and then took the
hand of the woman that Cassandra gauged to be about
her own age. Samantha appeared nervous and a little on
edge as she shook Doc's hand whereas the older man had
been poised and calm. It did not appear that they were
a couple since Samantha wore a wedding ring and the
older gentleman did not but Cassandra could not be sure.

"This is Cassandra. She will be sitting in with us, if
that is okay," said Doc to the two newcomers. Then to
Cassandra, he added, "Cassandra, this is Father Mallory
and Mrs. Pratt."

Cassandra shook the hand of Samantha and then the
priest. She had not noticed the collar beneath Father
Mallory's light jacket until she knew to look for it but his
presence there intrigued her. She had no idea what the
meeting was about or why a priest would bring a woman
to see Kaufler but she could tell it was serious.

"Please, let's have a seat and talk about what's
happening."

Father Mallory and Samantha sat down on the couch as Cassandra and Damien took their seats across from them in the armchairs. There was tension etched on Samantha's face that showed through in the tightness of her lips and the creases in her brow. She appeared haggard after she settled in and Cassandra noticed that she had bags under her honey-brown eyes that not even her makeup could hide.

"I don't know how to explain all of this," said Samantha as she looked to the priest.

"It's okay. They will understand. Doc is very good with this sort of thing."

Samantha exhaled deep and turned back to Damien. "I had my daughter, Lauren, seven months ago. She was a healthy baby, all was fine and we brought her home. Everything was great the first month but then I started noticing things in her nursery that were... strange."

"Can you tell me what sort of things you noticed?" asked Damien.

"Well, the first thing that happened was on the night that we put her down in her nursery. I went in to check on her because she had never slept through the night before where she hadn't cried once. When I went in, I found the bumper padding from around her crib lying in the floor."

Cassandra felt goose prickles go up her arms. She used a bumper pad for Sean when Peter insisted that his old crib had to go into the nursery. Her greatest fear with the old crib was that Sean would roll over in his sleep and get his head stuck between the slats. All of that changed when Laney saw the nursery and her fear of the slats was replaced with Laney's fear of Sean being suffocated by the baby bumper.

"The bumper, was it the kind that weaves through the corners of the crib or the one that ties on to each slat?" she asked.

"The tie one, my husband's mother gave it to us at the baby shower."

Cassandra nodded. "I had the same kind in my son's crib. My sister freaked out on me because there were some who said that the bumpers could be bad for kids."

"Yeah, there are all sorts of people who say that they were only needed for older cribs and now they're just a suffocation hazard. I didn't want one in our new crib but my mother-in-law insisted and, well…" she trailed off and shrugged.

"So, from the sound of it, I take it there's no way your daughter could have kicked this out?" asked Doc after he gave Cassandra a curious glance.

Cassandra and Samantha shook their heads in unison. It was at that moment that it dawned on Cassandra what that meant and what Samantha alluded to when she said 'strange.' *Please, tell me this is not what I think this is about,* she thought. She looked at Father Mallory in his priest's attire and beneath her calm exterior a shudder coursed through her. *Oh, no, this isn't really happening.*

"What happened next?"

"Things just started to happen. I was sitting up one night reading in the bedroom, which is right next door to the nursery. My husband was asleep next to me and all of a sudden, I heard what sounded like a man and a woman talking. I got up thinking that our Pomeranian had stepped on the remote on the couch and turned on the TV. That was when I realized that the voices were coming from the nursery. I woke my husband up and he went in but there was nobody in there."

"Do you live in a house or an apartment?"

"A house," answered Samantha. "There was nobody outside, either. I sent Tom out to make sure."

Father Mallory turned to face Samantha. "Tell him about the rest."

"At first, I started to think Tom was right, that I was just being paranoid about the baby being safe. I started talking to Father Mallory because my mother felt I might be suffering from postpartum depression. Then things started to happen that were unexplainable. When Tom's sister and husband would come over to see us, the door to the nursery would close and things would turn up in strange places. It was weird but we weren't sure if maybe we closed the door or something. Then, it just got worse."

"What do you mean worse?"

"Tom's sister and brother-in-law moved in with us for a while when their townhouse was remodeled. Sarah got hit one night when she went in to check on the baby, there was nobody in the back of the house but something blacked her eye. Then, Matt got bounced off of the walls in the hallway and had to go to the ER. Ever since then, there's a presence that is always around Lauren. You can feel it and with all that has been going on, it's driven a wedge between my husband and I. His family won't come over. I just... I want it to stop."

Cassandra did not know what to make of the woman's story. She did not believe in ghosts or poltergeists. Her belief was simple. God would not make a heaven and a hell for the souls of the dead to go to and then let spirits roam around of their own accord. She never bought into the whole idea that some people were afraid to go into the light, either. That did not add up with anything that she ever read in the Bible.

The one thing that Cassandra did believe in was demons. The Bible made it clear that they existed and could cause mayhem among the living, whether they could be seen or not. She was not sure why Samantha would have come to Damien Kaufler if it was a demonic presence, though. He was not a priest and the fact that the priest had brought her to him made her think that it had more to do with the woman's state of mind than something paranormal.

"In order for me to get a better understanding of what is going on, I will need to visit your home. Will that be okay?"

Samantha nodded, "I just want it to stop."

"Well, I will look into this for you. I can't tell you anything just yet; but, from everything I have heard thus far, it sounds like I may be of some assistance."

"I told her if anybody can get to the bottom of this, it would be you, Doc," said Father Mallory.

"Yeah, Father Mallory mentioned that you helped the Walkers. I did not know them but…at this point, I'm open to whatever remedies God provides, however, he provides it."

"Well, that's good," said Doc. "When could I come out and see the house?"

"How about Friday?"

"That sounds great. I will do whatever I can."

CHAPTER EIGHT

C assandra watched Kaufler shut the door after he showed Father Mallory and Samantha out. She had a million questions that she wanted to ask now that they were gone, but she was not sure where to begin. The whole meeting was weird and she never really understood what was going on that required his sort of assistance. For that matter, she did not have a clue what his assistance even was.

Kaufler paced through the pool house with his fist pressed to his mouth. It reminded Cassandra of the thinker statue sitting on the rock; only Kaufler was clothed and in no way seated. She hated to interrupt him as he pondered in the silent shuffle back and forth, but there was no way that he could expect her to sit there and be quiet.

"So, what was that? Did you major in Anthropology and minor in Psych?"

"No. I could have CE tested my way to a doctorate in psychiatry, though," he said with a laugh and then added as Cassandra looked at him confused. "My father liked to play a game he called 'Shrinkopardy.' It was his own unique version of the game show."

"Okay," she said with a wry smile. "Then what was all of that about?"

Doc walked back over and sat down in the armchair. "I'm not sure. Could be a battered wife in denial and it's easier to blame an entity than her husband."

"Do you think that may be it?"

"Not from what Father Mallory shared. He, too, experienced the presence."

"So, this is some ghost investigating stuff that you do?"

"Not exactly."

"Are you some sort of self-proclaimed psychic?"

Kaufler laughed. "There are cases of psychics, seers, mediums, and so forth throughout all cultures for centuries. I'm not one of them, though."

"Then what can you do for this woman that the priest can't? Why doesn't he perform an exorcism and go from there?"

"Well, according to Father Mallory, he tried to exorcise the spirit. It asserted its presence as he tried to banish it and it has manifested since then."

"What's that mean, then?"

"I don't know. I'll have to see what the house is like, where it is located and what its history is before I can even try to guess what's going on."

"So, wait, you think something is going on? Like a spirit can stand up to an ordained priest?"

"Something is going on, be it exoteric or esoteric," said Kaufler as he got up to pace once again. "And just because the mainstream world believes that the power of Christ is the absolute in spiritual matters, that does not necessarily mean his name or authority compels all things."

Cassandra cut her eyes at Kaufler. "That's ridiculous. How could God not compel all things?"

"That would depend, really, on which God stood in the God of Abraham's way," said Kaufler.

"God of Abraham? You mean the Lord, in the Bible!" said Cassandra. "No offense, Doc; but the gods of mythology don't count. They aren't real and you sound like you read too much online."

"For even if there are so-called gods, whether in heaven or on earth, as indeed there are many gods and lords," quoted Kaufler.

"I have never read that in my Bible."

"Pick up a copy that hasn't been stepped on with 'modern' fixes, and check out 1 Corinthians Chapter 8," he said. "The bottom line is your God, has gone to great lengths to be the one and only God. Every time that it states in the Bible, Talmud or the Qur'an that He is the one and only God, the biggest question never asked is why he ever had to say it in the first place."

Cassandra felt as if she had been struck. She wanted to argue with him but words would not come. It seemed that Louise might have been right as it was clear that he did not believe in the same thing that she did.

"Mr. Kaufler, as a Christian, I have to agree to disagree with you. I think that you have the wrong person for your books if that is what you want me to help you write."

"Have I offended you?"

"Little bit," she said. "I don't know how long you have been detached from the rest of the world, but in case you don't know, Christians do not believe the same things that Muslims do. In fact, the last I checked, I'm pretty sure that they view Christ as a mere prophet."

"Nice distinction," said Doc. "However, you're missing my point."

"Which is what? We all have it wrong?"

"That's not what I am saying ...."

"You just quoted the Bible and tried to patronize me and my faith with it," she said. "Do you understand what the word disparage means?"

Kaufler stopped in the middle of the room. He studied her for a minute with his ice-blue eyes and shook his head before he gestured toward the door. Cassandra followed after him and was glad that he did not debate it any further with her. It was awkward enough and she was trying hard not to be angry. Some people had a lot of nerve. How did he think that he could ask her for help and then talk about her God like that?

"If you change your mind, you know where to find me."

"Thank you, but I think I will pass," she said as she stepped out into the warm afternoon air. "I will have my boss run the piece that I wrote and leave out everything else."

"I appreciate that."

"Well, you have a good day."

The walk back through the mansion and then out to her car gave Cassandra time to cool off and think. She could not wrap her mind around how a man who seemed to be such a philanthropist could be so crass toward the beliefs of others.

It did not make sense to her. Yet, nothing about Kaufler made much sense to her. She didn't want to judge him and be the kind of person who held other's eccentricities against them; she knew that she had her own fair share of quirks that could likewise be judged, but she just did not understand Kaufler, or Doc, or whatever he liked to be called.

As she got into her car, she took one last look at the sign and sighed. Regardless of what his personal outlooks were, he was trying to help people. *As long as he continues to give shelter to those in need and leaves the beliefs of others alone,* she thought.

CHAPTER NINE

S tress was not something that Chris Sullivan showed on his face. It came through in the most subtle ways. The constant attempt to pop his knuckles, which he had already cracked, was a big clue. The need to remain standing was another. Cassandra knew her brother-in-law well enough to see that he was tense and when the Nerf football found its way into his hands, she knew that he'd been bottling up his anxiety by how the foam yielded under his grip.

"I don't know what to do, Cass," he said. "I listen. I hear her. I go and I check but there is nothing there. I can't combat shadows and things that don't really go bump in the night."

"We've talked, but I didn't know it was this bad."

"It's almost every night. I check on the boys, I make sure the security system is on, I check to make sure all the doors and windows are locked. There is nothing there. Nothing." The football would have suffocated had it been alive in his hands. He shook his head and went to speak but then shook his head again.

"I'll talk to her and see what is going on, Chris," she said. "It may be that she is not adjusting to the move or maybe, it is something else."

"Will you do that for me? I don't want her to feel like I am not taking her seriously, I believe that crazy stuff can happen. I've been in some bad situations and God's been there for me but this is just... this isn't the sort of thing I'm used to."

"Have you heard or felt anything?"

"I thought I saw someone upstairs and figured it was one of the boys. They were out back, though; and it was probably just a shadow from the sun passing behind a cloud or something," he said and put the football down. "Beyond that, I hear the fridge and air conditioner kick on; I hear the duck work in the attic expand whenever the air turns off; and I feel glad to be Stateside, in our home with my family."

Cassandra nodded. "I'll talk with her. It'll get better, Chris."

"Thanks," he said. "I hope so."

The first person that came to Cassandra's mind was Kaufler. She wondered if he could help but was reluctant to bring it up. He had helped people according to Father Mallory, even if he didn't see God the way that she did. Even if his method was to allay people's fears rather than to dispel ghosts, it could be what brought Laney some peace of mind.

"Hey, I might be able to talk to someone that could put her mind at ease if she is convinced that this place is haunted."

"Like a psychic or something?"

"Not really. On second thought, I shouldn't have brought it up."

"Hey, if it will help her get over this waking me up three and four times a night, talk to whomever you have to talk to. I mean, I really don't know what else to do, Cass."

"Okay. I will talk to her first and then we'll see if I need to do that."

"That'd be so awesome if you could help with this."

Cassandra assured him that she would and left him to the task of getting the grill out of the garage as she went back into the house to find her sister. She found Laney in the kitchen finishing up the salad that she was making and checked to see where her nephews were. Through the sliding glass door she saw that Kyle and Riley were both out in the backyard mustering up their forces of green army men; and from the look of Captain America in Kyle's hand and Iron Man in Riley's, she was sure that they were going to be a while.

"Do you need me to do anything?" she asked.

"Can you get out the bowls for me in the cabinet over there?"

Cassandra found the cabinet and pulled out five bowls. "Are you feeling any better now that you are getting settled in?"

Laney sighed and set to rinsing the potatoes that they were going to bake. "Not really. Why? Did Chris tell you how I have been waking him up?"

Cassandra shrugged. "What's been going on exactly?"

"Everything I told you before but now I've seen him," she said in a hushed whisper.

"Seen him?"

"Oh, yeah. I know it sounds like I'm out in left field somewhere; but there is a ghost in this house. And, it's like he's screwing with me. I don't know if I should be scared or annoyed or angry."

Cassandra could hear the sincerity in her sister's voice. Laney believed that the house was haunted. Whether she and Chris believed in ghosts didn't really matter. It was clear that Laney did. In the attic, lurking in the shadows of the basement or half in the wall with its face sticking out, thought Cassandra as she started to creep herself out. She decided to not do that anymore as she glanced around half anticipating seeing a misty face sneering at her for her disbelief.

"Are you sure that it's not the stress of feeling like you have all the unpacking to do and so forth?"

"Let me show you something."

Laney abandoned the baked potatoes that she had not yet wrapped in aluminum foil and led Cassandra into the dining room. A couple boxes sat on the table where their content had been emptied and placed in the hutch; and although the hutch was getting where Cassandra knew Laney liked it, the other boxes on the floor told her that there was more work to be done.

"You're making progress."

Laney laughed. "That is hilarious because yesterday, all of this got put in the hutch while the boys played and Chris was at work. I fixed lunch and came back... ta-dah."

"You're joking."

"Do I look like I'm joking?" asked Laney. Her straight face made Cassandra feel uneasy. "Oh, and that picture back there got hung up as well and it was centered even though I did it by myself. Where you see it is where I found it."

The frame for the enlarged black and white photo of an old timey kitchen was propped up against the wall in the way that Cassandra would have set it down so as to not have it tip. Cassandra knew there had to be an explanation. She knew Laney wouldn't make it up so that left the boys. Kyle and Riley had to be doing this even though they were more likely to leave their toys out rather than put them up, which made them doing this hard to believe, too.

"Are you sure that…"

"Cassandra," said Laney, cutting her off.

"Elaine."

"I am sure of what I'm sure of," she said. "The nail is right there on the table and the hole is right there in the wall."

"All right, I will go as far as saying that something is happening here that I don't understand. That does not mean that I am going to say it's a ghost."

"It is. I have got to do something, Sis."

"Well, I might know someone that I can talk to and get them to look into this. I can't guarantee it will help. In fact, I am pretty sure that this is going to be a mistake, but I will call later when I get home. Okay?"

"That would be excellent! Who is she? Is it that psychic that Nina told us about that one time?"

Cassandra shook her head. "No and we're not going talk about this anymore until I can talk to them about it, all right?"

"Okay, just promise you'll call tonight."

"I will," said Cassandra. "Oh, and maybe we can give Chris a break, let him sleep tonight. I don't have Sean so if you want I can stay here and take up ghost watch with you."

Laney gave a sheepish smile. "Ghost watch, makes me feel like we're in grade school again," she said and laughed. "He does have to go in early and I'd really like that."

"Then it's settled."

The two sisters hugged and then set to finishing with the dinner preparations. The silence that fell on the kitchen was occasionally broken by the rush of water from the faucet and the sound of clattering pots as the vegetables were put on the stove.

It was not uncomfortable even though Cassandra was still concerned about what was going on with Laney. The mood seemed to lighten when it became clear that she would stay the night and call someone who might be able to help. *God, please don't let this be a mistake*, she thought.

The sliding glass door opened and Chris popped his head in. "Those potatoes ready?"

"Oh, yeah, here they are."

"Here," said Cassandra as she stretched out her shirt to take them and gave Chris a nod toward Laney. "I will take them out and go make that call. You just put them on the grill same as always, right?"

"Yeah."

Cassandra made her way out onto the patio and headed for the grill. She knew when the sliding glass door closed that Laney was explaining what they had decided on. She was also sure that Chris would be relieved to know that something was about to give. As she dropped the potatoes onto the grill she heard Riley proclaiming victory for the forces of Iron Man followed by Kyle's adamant declaration that were it not for Captain America Iron Man would have lost.

"Boys," she called out. "Were you two on the same side?"

"Yes, Aunt Cass," they replied in unison.

"Did you two win?"

"Iron Man's troops took down Megatron and won the war," said Riley.

"Only after Captain America saw that Megatron was the bad guy."

"Everyone knows that Megatron is a bad guy…"

"Boys," said Cassandra. "How about we just celebrate that you two both won as a team?"

The reluctance that came with a shared win turned into excitement as a new development emerged. The enemy was not defeated, after all; and it had all been a clever ploy by some other action figure that was about to unleash the proto-something-or-other on the populace, which Cassandra surmised, had something to do with the water sprinkler they were repositioning around.

She shook her head and laughed before stepping off to the side of the house to make her call. The lady that answered at the Refuge put her on hold until she could get Doc on the line. She listened to the elevator music through several loops until the woman answered again and gave her the cell phone number that Doc could be reached at per his request. Cassandra thanked her and then hung up to dial the cell phone.

"Have you reconsidered?" answered Kaufler.

"Hi, Doc," she said and rubbed her neck. "I'm not calling about writing your story."

"Okay."

"Well, I guess in order to understand what you are doing I will have to shadow you as you put it but...."

"So, you've reconsidered disguised in a maybe?"

"Not exactly," she said. "My sister is convinced that her new home is haunted and you're, well, you."

"You don't believe in ghosts so you want to understand what I do, in order to feel comfortable asking me to help her?"

"That's one way of putting it."

There was a silence on the other end that stretched out for a lot longer than Cassandra liked.

"Okay, well, you can still make it to the Pratt's house. Do you have GPS?"

"Yeah."

"I'll get that address for you and we can go from there," he said. "As for your sister, I have no problem with helping regardless of what you decide to do; however, don't make a decision just yet. And, I will still pay you as I said before."

Cassandra was unenthusiastic about agreeing to that but at the same time he was willing to help her sister regardless of what she decided and he was still going to pay her. "All right, I will shadow you and we'll have to iron out all the other stuff but let's be clear on one thing, this is a trial basis. No more, no less."

"Agreed."

CHAPTER TEN

TENLEYTOWN, WASHINGTON, DC

Cassandra wanted to throw her GPS out the window by the time she pulled up to Samantha Pratt's brick bungalow. The directions that the device gave her had been all wrong. She spent half an hour going up and down Forty Third Street NW and then up and down Brandywine Street NW before she concluded that if it said recalculating one more time, it would be its last. She had decided to call Kaufler instead so that he could guide her in and unplugged the GPS before she hurled it out into oncoming traffic.

"Glad you could make it," said Kaufler from the sidewalk after she parallel parked. "How's your sister doing?"

"Better, she is hoping that the person I know might be able to help her out," she said, and then looked back at her car. "I should have met you at the Refuge and should have come over with you."

"That bad?"

"My GPS could not find this place, it was ridiculous."

"Well, good thing you called the other evening to let me know you'd reconsidered," he said.

Cassandra gave him an arched brow. "I'm glad I called. Had I gotten the address from Father Mallory to just show up, I'd have been so lost! Thanks for giving me your cell number through that lady at the front desk, too."

"No problem," he said. "Sometimes picking up a phone has its advantages."

Cassandra thought about how she chose to drive to the Refuge to confront him rather than call and knew that he was right about that. "So, how is this going to work? And, what am I supposed to call you?"

Doc flashed a playful smile. "Doc is fine. Just call me Doc. It's easier," he said. "And, how indeed?"

Cassandra knew that she would have to start thinking of him as Doc so that she wouldn't call him anything else. *Just try to remember that he likes Doc,* she thought; and then she said, "Hey, if I am to chronicle all this, I need to understand your methods."

"The method is simple. We go in and we see what happens."

"Really? Just like that?"

"No. Not just like that," said Doc as he shook his head. "There is no simple explanation. We go in and find out what there is to find out."

Doc gestured for Cassandra to go first in a gentlemanly manner. She was still not sure how she felt about him. He was weird, eccentric and made little sense to her but she had to admit that he had an underlying kindness to him.

The question that remained for her was what was it that he really did? And could he help Laney?

She walked up the brick steps and headed for the house. She knew that it was not the time to try to figure Doc out. Even if she could, she wasn't sure how it would even matter. *And, besides*, she thought, *this is good practice at being a journalist and taking notes.*

Samantha Pratt greeted them at the door. Her eyes looked drawn and tired and her hair was pulled back in the way that some women do when they do not have the time to fix it up. She gave them an exhausted smile and welcomed them in.

Doc entered the house with an air of humility and Cassandra noted that his eyes swept the foyer with keen interest. She did not know what he was looking for but wondered if he was searching for spirits. A smile began to spread on her face but she did her best to suppress it. She didn't want to appear to be making light of Mrs. Pratt's situation, especially when her thoughts had nothing to do with Mrs. Pratt.

Doc moved through the foyer without a word. His attention was not with either of them as he looked into the office on the right. She watched him with curiosity as he stopped and gave a slight raise of his eyebrows. He didn't enter the room but Cassandra could see that he looked over everything. *What is he looking for? Is there a way to tell if there's a ghost by looking at the room.*

She found herself looking at the space in an attempt to see what he saw. That proved difficult since she had no idea how he viewed it. All that she found was a room that had been converted into a study. There was a computer, a small television off to one side, a fax machine and a lot of clutter but nothing that struck her as important. It was an office area that was a lot like her own at home.

"Anything ever happen in there?" asked Doc.

"Yes," answered Samantha. "Sometimes it feels like I am being watched in there. My husband has also felt that there is a presence."

Doc nodded and then walked into the room. Samantha lingered in the foyer where Cassandra decided she wanted to stay. If there was a presence in the room, then she did not want to tangle with it. Doc could play around with forces that were beyond the realm of human understanding, but Cassandra was not about to be beside him if things got out of control.

"When do you experience these manifestations?"

"Late at night sometimes. Sometimes in the day."

"What are you doing when this presence makes itself known?"

"I am usually on the computer checking messages and playing one of my games."

Doc went to the computer and glanced back at them. "May I?"

Samantha nodded her consent and Doc pulled out the swivel chair to take a seat. He turned on the computer and after it booted up, he went online. "Any particular site that you visit?"

"There are some in my favorites. Mainly social networks for family and my Christian sites."

Doc asked if he could go into her favorites and then went to one of the sites that Cassandra herself watched with Sean. "This is a good one," he said. "I enjoy the music and the testimonies."

"You visit that site?" asked Cassandra. Her disbelief was evident.

Doc did not answer but instead typed in the name of a band. "What else is going on while you are doing this?"

Samantha arched her brow at Doc. "What do you mean?"

The music of Lifehouse began to play as Doc lifted his hands up and motioned around the room. "Do you sit down and check your messages during a break in your day? Do you have other things going on?"

"I usually sit down in-between tasks," she said. "Why?"

"Like, the dishwasher and other things are going on and you take a seat here while waiting?"

Samantha nodded.

"What is behind that wall, there?" Doc asked and pointed toward the back of the house.

"The kitchen."

"Hmm."

Cassandra was not sure what Doc was doing or why he got up all of a sudden but he was up on his feet and on the move. He murmured a polite excuse me as he passed them, and then took an immediate left. Cassandra followed after him with curiosity gnawing at her. Doc headed down the hall to the kitchen and took in the photos on the wall as he went. A genuine smile spread on his face when he passed the wedding photos.

He glanced back at Samantha. "You're happy in the photos."

"It was one of the best days of my life," she said. "Love was in the air."

Doc smiled deeper. "Love should always be in the air and if I may say so, you two look wonderful together."

"Thank you," said Samantha. "But, falling in-love is easy, Mr. Doc, staying in-love is another matter. Without God, I think my marriage would have already fallen apart."

"If he were ever married, he would understand," said Cassandra as Doc hung a right and entered the kitchen.

Doc gave her a blank stare as he moved into the kitchen which made her feel as though she had misspoken. He did not say anything but she thought she struck a nerve. She chose not to dwell on it and let it go. Instead she focused on the kitchen and how he examined the dishwasher, fridge and stove.

"Where is your breaker box?" he asked.

Samantha walked to the pantry door and opened it. "In here."

Doc stepped over and looked into the walk-in pantry. It was clear that he thought he had discovered something, but Cassandra was at a loss on what it might have been.

"So, you've got the dishwasher running, with the fridge and breaker box right here," he said as he gestured with his hands. "And there are a lot of electronics in the other room as well, which are on this side of the wall with the dishwasher, fridge and breaker box…"

"What do the electrical appliances have to do with it?" asked Samantha.

"EMF." said Doc. "EMF, or Electro-Magnetic Frequency. Anyone who watches ghost shows knows about EMF. It's one way of trying to debunk a 'presence' by seeing what kind of levels of EMF you have."

"Ghost shows?" asked Samantha. "I admit I watch more dramas than anything."

Cassandra nodded in agreement with Samantha. She did not watch anything that had to with paranormal investigations. She watched a few horror movies here and there but nothing that was about people trying to prove ghosts existed.

She saw advertisements for those sorts of programs and had to block one so that Sean didn't turn it on and scare himself by watching it; that was all she needed was a six year old terrified of ghosts.

"Yes, ma'am," answered Doc. "There are some that are very informative and great to watch, there are also others that aren't. It's not for everyone. However, I do think that you probably have a lot of EMF going on here."

"Can you find out for sure?" asked Samantha. "If it is what you said, EMF?"

"I can," he said. "I have an EMF detector out in my car. What I would like you to do is to run a load of dishes and turn on whatever you would normally while I go get it."

"Okay," said Samantha.

Cassandra watched Doc leave the room and decided to stay. She wanted to talk to Samantha alone and waited for the front door to shut before she approached the subject. "May I ask you a question?"

"By all means," answered Samantha as she prepared the dishwasher.

"How much is he charging you for this?" she asked. "I have someone that he might have to help and I kind of would like to get an idea. I'm sure that it's not the same for everyone, I'd like to know ballpark."

"Nothing."

"Nothing?"

"Father Mallory said that Doc never charges. He doesn't believe in it."

"Nothing? That's a little too good to be true isn't it? Where's the catch?"

"I thought you worked with him?"

"I do, sort of," she said. "I don't know him very well. We just met before meeting with you, so I am new to all of this."

"I trust Father Mallory," said Samantha. "Not to be rude, but I think that you're looking for a catch that's not there."

"Am I?"

"Whatever there may or may not be with Mr. Doc, he knows the truth and it is not my place as a Christian to judge him. Besides, Father Mallory would not have spoken on his behalf if he were a bad man."

Cassandra was stung by Samantha's words. How could she not wonder? Was she that blind? She let it go since she didn't want to be pushy but she was struggling to understand Doc's motivation.

When Doc returned with the EMF detector, she listened as he and Samantha talked about the ways EMF could affect a person. From nausea, to paranoia and feelings of being watched, even to hallucinations that could make the mind think it was seeing something that wasn't there. Cassandra did not know enough about EMF to know if what he was saying was true. She considered looking it up on her phone to get a better understanding of the subject but decided to wait and research it later. *It could be EMF that's gotten to Laney, if this is true,* she thought.

"Sitting right here, you are in a 7 to an 11mG," said Doc, his voice was serious. "It keeps fluctuating back and forth."

"What is unhealthy?"

"Healthy is considered to be around 2mG and under. But, tolerances depend on the person."

"Oh, my," said Samantha. "Can it hurt us?

"If you're sensitive to EMF, sitting here for a prolonged period of time could have you feeling like you are sick to your stomach and it could be producing that feeling of a presence like someone is watching you. High readings like this could cause someone to develop skin rashes if you are suspeticle to it."

"That sounds horrible. How do we fix that?"

"Well, before you start to worry, understand that I am not an expert on EMF. There are some who do not believe that it can harm us. However, our bodies and brains work on signals and currents. Sitting in an area like this that has high electromagnetic frequencies *could* contribute to what you are experiencing here. I don't know that it is, I'm saying that it could be a possibility."

"Well, what can we do to bring the levels lower?"

"Use less electrical appliances at once. Or, just be aware that this area here is a hot spot for high EMF when all of the appliances in the kitchen are in use," he said. "You might also want to talk to an electrician to find out if your wiring is up to code."

"What about when we are in the back of the house where I have heard voices talking?"

"That is where we should go next."

Cassandra followed Doc and Samantha down the hall. They passed the kitchen and dining room on the left and right, and ventured into the back of the house where the bedrooms were. There were more photos on the hall's wall and seeing the Pratt family made Cassandra smile. Then she recalled the tension that was among the family and hoped that Doc was not a fraud. If he could help them regain their love and peace, then perhaps whatever he believed in was not so bad and perhaps he was a decent man as she had originally believed.

Doc asked to see the baby's bedroom and Samantha showed them in to the nursery. Cassandra loved the motif that Samantha had chosen. The walls were done in rainbows and there were adorable animal stickers everywhere on the walls. A cartoonish lion played with a group of mice on one wall and on another there was a frog dancing on a pelican's beak.

"This is a cute room."

Samantha turned to Cassandra. "Thank you."

Doc sat down in the middle of the floor and crossed his legs Indian style. "This is where you hear the voices?"

"Yes, this is where I have heard the voices."

"So, the baby bumper was out here in the floor and your in-laws got attacked?"

"Yes. The baby-bumper was right there in the floor," Samantha pointed. "The rest took place out in the hall.

Doc set the EMF detector down on the floor. The reading was down in the point zeros from what Cassandra could read. She did not understand what they were supposed to be doing and the longer Doc sat there, the more impatient she became.

"What did these voices sound like, again?"

"One was a female voice, the other a male voice."

"What are you thinking, Doc?" asked Cassandra.

"Could it have been something that you thought you heard in a light sleep?" asked Doc.

"No. It was very clear that it came from this room."

Doc got up and looked out the window. There was a house not too far away even though there was a privacy fence that separated the yards. Cassandra knew that if there were anyone outside smoking a cigarette and talking, that the voices could have travelled and sounded like they came from the nursery. She wondered if that is what Doc would conclude. If he strung this woman along and had her believe that it was a ghost, she was going to be ticked.

Cassandra watched Doc as he shook his head and shuddered. "Mrs. Pratt, if you would be so kind may I have a few minutes to confer with Mrs. O'Neal?"

CHAPTER ELEVEN

"Wait a minute, what are you saying?"
Doc held Cassandra's gaze as he lifted his eyebrows in a disarming expression. "There is a presence in this room and it is not evil."

"How can you know that?"

"Call it a guess."

Cassandra crossed her arms over her chest. "This is too much," she said with aggravation. "You're not even picking anything up with the EMF detector."

"What is in here or I should say what was in here is not something we would pick up with an EMF detector."

"So, what is it then?"

"If I'm right, I think it might be a guardian."

Cassandra did a double take. "Excuse me?"

"A guardian? An angel? A being of light that walks with us through life, assigned to us by God?" he said.

"I thought that you did not believe in my 'Abrahamic' God?"

Doc shook his head. "I never said that I didn't believe in your God. In fact, I am pretty sure I never said what I believed."

"You said that God is not the *one* and *only*. I recall that clearly because I kind of wanted to hit you," she said. "I know, not very Christian of me, but it was more how you said than what you said. You also quoted a scripture that I'm pretty sure you're interpreting wrong 'to your own destruction.' That is in the Bible somewhere, too!"

Doc's hands came up. "I apologize for making you want to hit me," he said. "Sometimes I say things that I assume people will understand what I mean…"

"Oh, I understood perfectly," Cassandra interjected. "You disrespected my faith as well as the respectable faiths of millions of people in this world. Where I grew up, that's a lot like playing with fire, Mr. Kaufler, and God is a fire that will not cease burning."

"I meant no disrespect to you, or anyone. Can we clear the air?" asked Doc after a moment. "Allow me to apologize to you for being uncouth. Understand that I believe all the Gods that are out there are in some way real and deserve respect. I do not seek to disrespect you or your God. Nor do I seek to disrespect anyone else's God. That was not what I meant when I spoke in the pool house and I'm sorry for angering you."

"How could you have meant it any other way?" she asked.

"I meant it as an analogy to not be narrow-minded. I have no problem with God, Christ or Abraham. I have no problems with Atheists, Buddhists or Agnostics. Everyone is entitled to their belief and view. I may not agree or believe as you do, but I think that coexistence is paramount to our being able to get along and function as human beings."

"Saying that you believe in coexistence and respecting other people's beliefs is not how it sounded to me. What if I had chosen to not turn the other cheek and instead decided to send your words to the printer for all to read? What would you have done then?"

"That would have been an ethics violation; and I would have probably figured out whether I wanted to sue you or just try to explain that what I said was not supposed to be disrespectful," he said with a shrug. "Since I am not in the business of suing, I guess it'd have been the latter."

"Wow. You're something else, Doc."

"Hey, I'm sorry. I didn't mean to make you angry and I didn't mean to disrespect your belief or God," Doc said with a sincere tone. "I'm sorry. Can we focus on what's going on here?"

Cassandra crossed her arms and stood there for a moment unsure of what to do. Standing up for her beliefs and talking about God made her feel better, yet she also knew that she hadn't been a great example of a Christian lately. Looking at Doc made her realize just how far away from him she was. When had she last been to church? When had she last picked up a Bible? She could not remember. The truth was that she wore a cross but it had been a while since she honestly thought about what Christ had done at Calvary.

As she stood there, Cassandra remembered how her pastor used to encourage the congregation to think of Christ when the time came to forgive someone. She brought to mind Jesus hanging from the nails in his hands and feet, with the crown of thorns shoved down onto his head and the lacerations from the scourge covering his body. Every breath a labor of pain as the bones in his feet had to press down onto the nail so that he did not suffocate on his own shoulders. Every excruciating minute where there was nothing to quench the pain and knowing that he had to endure a bit longer. Yet, Christ's love was to look at the people who had sentenced him to die in such a horrific way and pray to his father that he would forgive them.

Cassandra knew that she needed to ask forgiveness for herself. The best that she could do was a quick silent prayer. *Dear Lord, forgive me for not being the best Christian that I can be and forgive me for my sins. Thank you, Father, for putting this man in my path to show me how far I have strayed. Amen.*

"I forgive you."

"Huh?" asked Doc. "You forgive me?"

"Yes, I forgive you. That doesn't mean that you're off the hook with God, though," she said.

It was clear that Doc did not know how to respond to her last statement. She could see him thinking about what should come next.

"Thank you?" he said after a moment. "Can we focus now?"

Cassandra couldn't help but smile at his question. "You're welcome. Now, about this guardian," she said. "What makes you think that it's a guardian angel?"

"I don't know how to explain it."

"Do your best."

"It's more of an uneducated guess," he stammered and grimaced.

"You sounded like you knew it was here."

Doc nodded. "I did. It's not what you'll think, though. I don't see ghosts or anything like that."

Cassandra crossed her arms once again. "Then what is it?"

"It walked through me, over there by the window. It walked through me," he said. "As it did I knew that it meant us no harm. It felt compassionate and kind but it wanted us to leave. Like, now."

Cassandra did not know what to say. "Is that how this usually works?"

"Not really," he said. "Most of the time I study what is going on and then figure it out like a puzzle. There have been a few instances where I couldn't explain something but I have never had an entity walk *through* me."

"Ghosts and possessions are real, then?"

Doc nodded. "As real as the equipment that captures them and the possessed bodies that contort under their influence."

"How can you know these things and still not call on Christ?"

"What I have encountered gives me pause," said Doc. "That is not what we need to worry about, though. Whatever was here isn't hostile."

"So, what attacked the brother and sister-in-law?"

"Maybe another entity that the guardian angel is here to protect against? I don't know."

"This is not my area of expertise. I am more lost on this than I was earlier," admitted Cassandra.

"That'd make two of us," he said. "I need to go back to the pool house to do some research."

Cassandra nodded understanding and let Doc lead the way out through the house. They found Mrs. Pratt busying herself in the office where she was organizing the desks paperwork. Despite their abrupt need to leave, Samantha remained hopeful that they were closer to supplying her with answers. Doc assured her that he would do his best and even though Samantha did not seem to notice, Cassandra could tell that he was rattled.

The walk out to their cars was silent and hurried. Doc stared at the ground in front of him as he made his way down the steps and as Cassandra attempted to catch up to him she almost stumbled. He stopped and made sure that she was okay and that was when she saw the look in his eyes.

"Hey, you're not scared are you?"

He shook his head and tried to play it off with a chuckle. "No."

"Wait," she said as he turned to walk to his car. "You're shaking, Doc."

He looked down at his trembling hands and made a fist. "I'm fine, really."

"Are you?"

"Okay, maybe it's not every day that you have something walk through you but the faster I can understand what I am dealing with in there, the better I will be."

"All right," she said and raised her hands.

They separated and Cassandra got in her car. As she sat there with her hands on the steering wheel waiting for Doc to go, she knew that whatever had happened in the house distressed him more than he was letting on.

She didn't know what to make of it. He believed that it was a good entity and she prayed to God that it *was* a guardian angel. *Yet, what kind of work is God doing through him?* There were too many questions and not enough to go on. For now, she had to trust in Christ and pray; and now, even more than ever, she knew that she needed to get back into church.

CHAPTER TWELVE

There was no end to the traffic as Doc neared the exit to the Refuge. Cassandra was glad to see that they were close and decided to smoke her last cigarette while she talked to her sister with the Bluetooth. At some point, she knew that she was going to have to stop and get gas as well as a pack of cigarettes. She just hoped that she had enough in her checking account to cover both.

"...when are you going to find out when your ghost guy can come out here?"

"I don't know, I will find out when I get a moment. I'm kind of in the middle of something, though. He did ask how you were doing."

"Things have kind of quieted down here, to be honest. Hold on," said Laney and the phone rustled, followed with a long pause. "Now, I swear I turned the dryer on and had all my jeans in the washer with it on."

"Are you sure?"

"Yeah, but I see what happened," she said. "Chris must have pulled them out and thrown them in the dryer and tossed the stuff that was in the dryer over into the basket. No need for alarm. It's normal stuff."

"Good," she said. "Although a ghost that does laundry wouldn't be such a bad thing."

"Don't say that," said Laney.

"Sorry."

Cassandra was glad to hear that things had quieted down for Laney. She hoped that meant it had just been the stress of moving in and dealing with everything that came with it. Yet, for all she knew, the spirit at Laney's could have hit a lull. *Now, I'm starting to buy into all of this.*

"Pray that it stays quiet," said Laney.

"Oh, I am. Trust me, I am. Well, I'm going to have to let you go because I am about to pass a gas station and I need to stop."

"Okay, enjoy the rest of your day and drop in later if you don't work late."

"Okay, I have to pick up Sean first, but we'll try to get out there."

Cassandra pulled into the gas station knowing that Doc would continue on without her. To her amazement she watched him hang a left as she pulled up to the pump and he drove around to pull into the other entrance of the gas station.

Doc maneuvered his Ford to the pump opposite of Cassandra and got out with a smile. "Hey, I think we have met before."

"I didn't think you'd see me pull in."

"I couldn't pass up $3.17 a gallon."

"God willing, it will stay this low or get lower."

"That would be nice," said Doc. "I was thinking about the Pratt's, I want to research more on this to be sure that what I experienced is what it was, but what if the bumper was all that the guardian had anything to do with? What if it is what I said earlier, that the angel is protecting the baby from another aggressive spirit that attacked the brother and sister-in-law?"

"Like an angel and a devil on the shoulders, but not, sort of situation?" asked Cassandra.

"Exactly."

"The other alternative is that the brother and sister-in-law are like you said before, in denial about their being in an abusive relationship. Maybe the Pratt's don't know."

"He got bounced off of walls, though. She got punched in the face."

"Maybe he hit her, and maybe she bounced him off the walls."

Doc pondered on that one for a moment. "Does that sort of thing happen? Are there guys who get beat up by their wives?"

Cassandra shrugged. "Sure there are. Do you not watch television?"

"I don't have much time for television," Doc admitted.

Cassandra's pump kicked off and she hung up the nozzle. "I am going in to get some smokes, I will meet you at the Refuge."

"I'll see you there."

Cassandra stood in line at the gas station and with all of the talk of guardian angels and spirits she considered where she was at in her relationship with God. Her spiritual life had not been there since she and Peter separated. It was not that she went out of her way to sin; she just had not gone out of her way to connect with him. She had stopped going to church to avoid seeing him there and she knew that a part of her pushed God away because Peter had stepped out on her. After a while, she could see where she shut God out completely.

The infidelity still hurt because despite all the things that Peter put her through, she still loved him. He had been such a sweet and loving man when they first married and then it all went south. Over time he paid no attention to her needs; he became a selfish jerk that didn't want to go out with her; every day he walked around like he had this huge chip on his shoulder and made her feel like it was all her fault.

How could he have done that to her? She loved him. She would have done anything for him and he threw their love away like it didn't even matter. She knew that it was not her fault. She was amazing and there were all sorts of men who had crushes on her and thought that he had been such an imbecile. That did not matter, though. She did not want to be with random men who had crushes on her and she did not want to be with the guy friends that told her how amazing she was, either. She wanted to be with Peter.

The line in front of Cassandra moved and she stepped forward. Her heart ached for a renewed relationship with God. Suddenly she missed him. She had missed him for a long time, too. God did not disappoint. He never walked out. He always listened and his answers were blessings. He never gave half-truths, exaggerated stories and gave excuses. God was the Truth and he was the Word.

The reality that her heart was heavy and alone made Cassandra almost well up in the middle of the gas station. She didn't know what else to do except give it to God and hope that whatever he had going on in her life he would take the feeling and replace it with happiness.

"How may I help you?" asked the cashier as Cassandra stepped up to the counter.

Cassandra fumbled with her wallet and glanced up as the voice behind the counter registered. "Isaac? Is that you?"

Isaac smiled his radiant smile. He was still as handsome and clean cut as he had been when she knew him at Peter's law firm, but he did not have the suit and tie that she was used to seeing on him. "Wow, you look amazing, Cass. How have you been?"

"Thank you!" Cassandra beamed. "I'm fabulous. I didn't expect you to be behind the counter."

Isaac lifted his hands. "Me neither but it's a job, isn't it?" he said.

Isaac's smile never wavered and that made his attitude all the more contagious. He had been one of the sweetest men that Peter had ever invited over to their house from the law firm. His manner was calm and collected but he had a certain carefree quality to him that she had liked.

"You are not at the law firm anymore?" she asked.

"No, I'm afraid that they had to let me go," he said and shrugged. "God is good, though. I got this job and a second one that I go to after I clock out here. Same hours at nowhere near the pay but Eisha and I manage."

"Hey, it's nice you two can catch up and all but we've got stuff to do."

Cassandra glanced back at the line. "Sorry. It's my fault."

"Lady, I don't care whose fault it is, get his number and talk later."

"Isaac, let me get two packs of Camel's, please," she said, not letting the man behind her ruin her newfound mood.

Isaac got the cigarettes and rang it up as Cassandra borrowed his pen. She jotted down her number on an excess piece of receipt and handed it to him before taking the packs.

"You and Eisha should stay in touch."

"She would love to see you again and get you back over to our church."

"Have her call me, then."

"I will. Have a wonderful day!"

"You, too."

Cassandra stepped out of the gas station and into the afternoon with a major smile on her face. She walked across the covered concrete area, passed the pumps and then climbed into her car before she even realized that Isaac had not told her what happened that caused the law firm to let him go. Peter had never mentioned it, either. And it hadn't crossed her mind to ask Isaac if they still talked.

The drive to the Refuge did not seem to take any time at all. Cassandra knew that half an hour had elapsed but her run in with Isaac had her in such a good mood that she sang to the windshield and drummed on the steering wheel. The one guy that cut her off did not even bother her. She was rocking out and having fun; and she wasn't about to let an aggressive driver get to her.

Cassandra did not find Doc in the pool house where she expected he would be. She saw his car was off to the side and decided to knock louder but no answer came. At last, she decided to pull out her phone and text him.

Where r u? she texted.

N the library. Where r u? replied Doc.

By the pool house. Library next to the theater?"

Yep.

K.

Cassandra left the pool house and made her way to the pool house. She went in through the door where she had first left the mansion to find Doc. Inside she found Oscar reading the paper while drinking a glass of orange juice. He glanced up and smiled at her with that sincerity he had that she found to be an inspiration.

"Afternoon, Mrs. O'Neal. It's good to see you again."

"It is good to see you, too, Oscar. And, please, call me Cass."

Oscar smiled and gave her a nod of gratitude. "I liked the article you wrote. Very moving."

"Thank you," said Cassandra. "Did I do your story justice?"

"Well, yes," chuckled Oscar. "There was one thing that I noticed, though."

"What's that?"

"You didn't mention that the Refuge helped me get my diabetes in check."

"I am so sorry, Oscar. I forgot," she said.

"Don't get all sentimental on me now. It didn't hurt my feelings any," he chuckled. "Besides, the miracle is in the fact that I don't have diabetes anymore. Written in the paper or not, it's something big."

"You're right about that."

"How've you been, working with Doc?"

"Did he tell you I was working with him?"

"No. I just wondered how it's going."

The question startled Cassandra. It wasn't a stretch that Oscar would have figured out that she was working with Doc. The man had seen a thing or two in his lifetime. Plus, Oscar reminded her of that older man that sat on the front porch reading the paper and drinking his juice that almost every neighborhood had. They never missed much.

Regardless of how sweet Oscar was Cassandra was still reluctant to answer because she knew that Doc liked his privacy. "I'm sorry, Oscar," she said and shrugged.

"If you can't answer, that is okay," he said. "Speaking of jobs, a man called here and said that he was with Holy United Church and after reading the article in the paper, he wanted to offer me a job if I was interested."

"That is fantastic, Oscar. I am delighted for you!"

"Delight in God, Sweetheart. Delight in God."

Cassandra knew that he meant it. She did not know why God's work was appearing everywhere she looked, but it was marvelous and humbling all at once.

Cassandra gave Oscar a hug and they parted ways better from the encounter. It felt good to be among people who loved and enjoyed the pleasure of life. Who were not so beaten down by life's hardships that they ceased to enjoy the moments that God provided them with.

As she made her way down to the library, it occurred to Cassandra that God may or may not have been working through Doc. That was something that she needed to discuss with a pastor to get a better understanding on.

She did not know how a non-believer could have God work good acts through him when he admitted that he did not believe in God as she did. What Cassandra was certain of, though, was that God was using Doc to open up her own eyes.

"There you are," said Cassandra as she stepped into the library.

"Here I have been," answered Doc with a light-hearted laugh.

"Sorry I took so long, I stopped to talk with Oscar," she said. "He is such a nice guy. He even called me Sweetheart."

Doc shook his head and laughed. "That's Oscar for you."

"He's a great guy."

"One of the coolest guys I know," said Doc. "He has more of a story than just how God has helped him through losing his home and his job, though. You should ask him about it some time."

Cassandra gave Doc a quizzical glance, but all he did was smile and point at the books that were laid out on the table and then pull out the seat next to him for her. She took the seat and looked at the books that Doc was examining. There was one on angels specifically Cherubim, Seraphim, Malachim, and some other names that she did not recognize.

"What have you found?"

"We will be here for a while."

"What do you mean?"

"See these listings," asked Doc as he pointed to the concordance. "We have these to read and we have these other books to look through as well."

"Why not pull it up online?"

"Because, I'd like to get the hard part done and save the easy part for last," he said. "Besides, when was the last time you sat down and studied?"

"It has been a while," she admitted. "Okay, what can I work on, then?"

"Here," he said and slid a Bible over to her. "Have at it. Everything that you can find on angels, guardians and messengers of the Lord is what we need."

Cassandra looked down at the Bible as Doc got up. It had been too long since she had cracked open her Bible. She bowed her head. *Dear God, forgive me for having turned away from you and neglecting my relationship with you. Thank you for this opportunity to see your works all around me and help me as I read your word. In Jesus' name I pray, Amen.*

Cassandra opened her eyes and found that Doc stood next to her with a large book in his hand. When she glanced up at him he gave her a polite smile and sat down.

They spent the next three hours poring over all of the material in the library that had to do with angels. Cassandra knew more about angels, their rank and all of the different kinds than she had ever even thought of before. She was just as fascinated by the legends of them as she was the biblical accounts. None of them were beings to be toyed with. And she had to admit that although she did not believe in the other religions that spoke of angels even when they called them by different names, she could understand why Doc felt that they deserved respect.

"As you can see, I think we've narrowed it down to a guardian angel or some sort of celestial being that's taken an interest in this family," said Doc before he drank from his water bottle.

"So, you feel no closer to understanding what is there than I do?"

Doc smiled and took a second drink before he put the lid back on the bottle. "I have never encountered anything quite like this."

Cassandra got up and showed Doc her pack of smokes and lighter. He acknowledged her unspoken request to smoke and they headed out of the library to go upstairs. Doc stopped her as she turned to go toward the stairs and directed her down through the theater where an exit led up to the back of the grounds out of sight of the back porch.

The fresh air was a nice change after being in the library for the last few hours. Cassandra had been craving a cigarette for the last two hours, but she had chosen to chew gum so that they could tackle the amount of reading that they had to do.

She fired up a cigarette as Doc leaned against the wall and considered what they knew about the entity in the house. "Tell me what it was like when the entity passed through you."

Doc closed his eyes. "I was standing there and then all of a sudden it was like I stepped outside from the AC into the summer afternoon. I was not in a cold spot or what I would call a hot spot, but I became warm. My entire body tingled, similar to when a limb falls asleep yet I felt awash in peace. There was no fear. I felt safe. Secure."

"How did the entity tell you that it wanted us to leave and how did you know that it wasn't hostile to us."

"I saw an image flash in my thoughts of a dove accompanied with the feeling one has when meeting a friendly person and then an image of two people shaking hands overpowered the first image. That is how it imparted that it was not hostile," explained Doc. "Then, the next image was hard to take any way other than it wanted us to leave. I saw an image of an *exit* sign accompanied with the feeling of having somewhere else that I needed to be."

Cassandra took in the description and exhaled a plume of smoke. "The entity felt good, though?"

"Well, yeah. It didn't feel evil."

"What if it is not a guardian angel? What if it is a fallen angel?"

"I dare say that Father Mallory has sufficient enough faith to rebuke a fallen angel."

Cassandra was glad that Doc said that. It opened the door for her to ask some more questions that had been gnawing at her ever since she spoke to the priest. "If he can rebuke a fallen angel, then why couldn't he rebuke the entity that possessed the boy that brought you and him together in the first place?"

Doc fixed his gaze on Cassandra. "Because, that entity was powerful and the priests were not prepared for it."

"What was it?"

"Not what but rather whom," said Doc. "His true name is lost in the centuries but based on what I saw and what he answered to, I called him Rove. He wouldn't speak in the languages of this age but from the way he laughed at the priest I think he knew their words well enough."

"Rove?"

"Yes, that's the best way to describe what I saw."

"Was he a demon?"

Doc shrugged. "He was a lost entity that was as much trapped as the boy that he possessed but I don't know that he was a demon," he said. "He wasn't evil. He was just tortured and needed some compassion and mercy. Most of all he needed some regard from the living. I don't know that he even enjoyed the pain and the helplessness that he was inflicting on the boy and his family. It seemed to me that he just identified with it."

"How did you communicate with it?"

"I put my hands on the kid's forehead while the priests held him down. From there, I saw images that came out in waves. It'd be like being on a beach at high tide, with a raging storm of animosity, anger, and pain attacking the shore."

Cassandra had long since put out her cigarette and stuffed it into the pack but as she listened to Doc's account she decided to relight it. "You saw it like you saw the images from the entity at the Pratt's house?"

"Yes and no," answered Doc. "I had to put my hands on the child's forehead to discover Rove and what I saw was a blur of rage and angst. There was nothing focused with Rove. The entity at the Pratt's just walked through me and I saw what I did."

"I thought you said you weren't psychic?"

"I'm not. I dream things from time to time that happen. In certain instances I can lay my hands on a person and see what's connected to them on the other side. It is not an exact science nor is it something that I understand."

"That is why you approach it all from a scholarly point of view, isn't it? You are afraid of your gift," she said.

Doc looked away and stared at the ground. "I was in India on a two week retreat when I had my first dream. The dream was of my father telling me that it was not logical for me to think that I was unique because all people are similar and yet special in their own right. He also said that he had something new that he wanted me to look at. A few nights later, I dreamt that they, my parents, were talking to me and telling me not to feel alone, but all I could see were their feet from beneath the car as if I were lying down on the opposite side of it looking at them."

Cassandra felt her heart sink. "Did you get to see them before the wreck?"

"Yes. I got to see them and I saw the car that dad wanted to show me," he said with a sad sigh. "I didn't even think anything of it until after the accident."

"You couldn't have known the dream would come true," she said. She looked him in the eyes and saw that they were a soft shade of sky-blue right then and that tears threatened to spill out onto his cheeks.

The man that she thought was a fraud and a hoax was proving to be a good-hearted man who just had a not-so-normal life. *His 'gift' is a little bizarre*, she thought. Yet, she could understand it in her own way.

"Let's not start digging up the past," said Doc after a thoughtful silence. "I remember it and that is enough."

CHAPTER THIRTEEN

The apartment was quiet as Cassandra opened the door and tossed her keys on the side table. A light was on in the back of the house that she guessed she had forgotten to turn off, but she gave it no more thought as she headed down the hall to put on some comfy clothes.

She was worn out after her day with Doc. There had been way too much packed into a single day. She was ready to relax and found herself in the mood to watch a movie. She approached Sean's room and had to remind herself that he was not there. He was at his Dad's for the rest of the week and she was on her own.

Out of habit, she looked into the room as she walked by. She knew that she would see his bed made, the Batman nightlight off and all the stuffed toys piled up against his pillow. The one she knew that she would not see was the Incredible Hulk that he had gotten for Christmas. It was his favorite gift and he carried it everywhere he went. He did not even know much about the Incredible Hulk, it was the fact that his Grandfather got it for him that made it his favorite.

To her surprise, the room was not empty. Sean was in bed and had his Incredible Hulk in a headlock. His nightlight was not turned on and made the room dark, yet she could make out her son in the bed as clear as day. She was confused. Were her eyes playing tricks on her?

From the end of the hall where she had come, a throat cleared and she jumped as she slammed her hand over her mouth. She turned to find Peter standing at the end of the hall biting his lips so that he did not laugh, while holding his hands up with that look of fear that she might be upset.

Cassandra abandoned going to get into comfy clothes and moved toward Peter.

"What are you doing here?"

"Sean did not want to stay at my place anymore, he doesn't want to be there when Kyla comes over," explained Peter. "I used the spare key you gave me for emergencies."

"I see," said Cassandra. "Let's take this to the back deck where I can smoke."

Peter went with her to the back deck and Cassandra lit up a cigarette as soon as she stepped out onto the balcony. Peter leaned against the rail and crossed his arms as she exhaled and Cassandra knew that she was going to have to talk to him about Kyla.

"Peter, he doesn't like Kyla because she says things about me that hurt his feelings."

"Excuse me? Do what?" asked Peter. "She wouldn't do that."

"He told me that she says mean things all the time. That you and Kyla do."

"Cassandra, I promise that we go out of our way to not speak negative about you in any way around Sean. We agreed that we would not badmouth each other, remember?"

"Yeah, like you agreed to cherish and to hold, for richer or poorer and in sickness and in health?"

Peter shook his head and threw his hands up. "Cassandra, I made a mistake. It was a huge mistake, and I am sorry about that but that was then. Right now you're telling me that our son does not want to spend time with me because Kyla speaks ill of you. I can't see that. When she is over, I never hear her say anything bad."

"He told me that you and Kyla both have said 'bad words' about me."

Peter looked up and searched the night air. Cassandra knew that he was trying to remember. He usually had so much on his mind that he forgot details that other people retained. He started to shake his head and she knew that he was coming up with nothing.

"The only thing that I can think of is that he overheard us discussing a case," he said. "That is all I can think of."

"Really? A case? You expect me to believe that?"

"It's the truth."

"Peter, not to be too skeptical but you are the one that denied having an affair until I caught you red-handed. You denied being involved with Kyla after we were separated. Why should I believe you?"

"I am not with Kyla, Cassandra. I have never even slept with her. She sits second chair with me at court. Sometimes Alonzo sits second chair and comes to my house, he's one good-looking Latino dude but when he crashes on my couch that does not mean that I have taken a liking to men."

Cassandra turned away from Peter and focused on smoking her cigarette. She did not know what to believe with Peter. He was a lawyer. "So, you deny it still?"

"Deny what?"

"That you and Kyla spoke ill of me in front of Sean? There was also a lesson in there about how poop-head was not a bad word, too."

Recognition dawned on Peter. "Oh, crap. Yeah, I know exactly what he is talking about," he said. "The Cassandra Sims case."

"Explain," she said as she crossed her arms.

"I had a client that sued another woman named Cassandra. We were going over our arguments at the table and I dropped the f-bomb when I realized that I had left half of the argument at the office on my desk. I think Kyla saw Sean and said 'Hey, don't be a poop-head' so that I'd know he was in the room or something to that effect. It never even crossed our minds that he believed that we were talking about you."

Cassandra had to admit that it sounded plausible but she was not sure what to believe. She wanted to believe Peter because then that would have meant that both he and Sean were right. There was still the matter of Kyla telling Sean that poophead was not a bad word. Cassandra did not know her well enough to be comfortable with her teaching her son what was good and bad.

"I will have to take what you say on faith. As difficult as that is, I can do that," said Cassandra. "What I can't do is have a woman that I don't know teaching our son that it is okay to say poophead."

Peter laughed a little and then covered his lips with the back his fingers to hide it. "Sorry," he said. "Poophead is a little over the top isn't it? If we teach him that poophead is okay to say, then he may graduate to worse later. I get it, I do."

"I am glad that you get it," said Cassandra as she fired up another cigarette. "I have been trying to get him to stop using it and I worry that he will call one of the kids in class poophead and get a red card."

Peter looked at the cigarette and scratched his head. "I thought you were never going to pick those back up?"

"I did, too," she said as she looked at the cigarette. "I don't even know where I picked them back up at to be honest with you. Just the other week I was declining a cigarette and now I am smoking like a chimney."

"You sound stressed."

"I am. There is all this stuff going on at work, I have a gazillion things that I need to be doing, but I am too busy to get it all done. I should have cleaned up the house while you had Sean, but I wasn't even here," she said. "The bright side is that I've felt God's presence in my life again for the first time since before we, well, you know..."

"Separated?"

"Yes. That," she said, then put the cigarette out on the banister after she gave it a thoughtful look. "I don't need that complicating matters."

Peter shook his head and smiled. "It sounds like you are dealing with a lot."

"I ran into Isaac," she said, changing the subject as she remembered to be thankful to have her problems. "You never mentioned that he got fired."

Peter looked away for a moment and then returned to her gaze. "A lot of people at Mossberg and Higgins have been let go. They've downsized considerably."

"The way this economy is, downsizing scares me," she admitted as she thought about the offer Hal got for the paper. "One thing that seeing Isaac did for me was help me see that no matter what happens, God will provide a way."

"He always does."

"Have you been going to Mass lately?" she asked and gestured to the door.

"No. I went five months ago and decided it was my last," he said as he opened the door for her.

"What did your parents have to say about that?" she asked as she passed him and stepped into the apartment.

"Dad was very calm and collected about it. So was mom. Neither of them seemed all that surprised. All they want is for me to figure out what I believe and to find a place of worship that I enjoy," he answered as they made their way into the living room.

Cassandra sat down on the couch and Peter sat down opposite of her in the recliner. She laid the cigarettes down on the coffee table and decided to pray God would give her the strength to not pick them up anymore. She could not believe that she was a smoker again. What would her son think if he saw her with a cigarette in her mouth? He had never seen her smoke and the example that she tried to set was not one of a smoker.

That was when it hit her. It was like a bucket of water thrown in her face and it came in the form of words that she had not read in too long a time. Why do you look at the speck of sawdust in your brother's eye and pay no attention to the plank in your own eye? She knew that she was mad at Peter for letting Kyla teach Sean poophead but she also knew that she cursed like a sailor herself. How many times had he been in the room opposite of her and heard her use vulgar language on the phone? How many times had she cursed the computer with him somewhere in the house? Had he heard her use curse words?

She put a hand to her head and said, "Oh, no."

"What's wrong?"

"I am just thinking about what a foul mouth I have while wondering how often I have said things where Sean could hear it."

"I wonder the same thing, all the time," admitted Peter. "When you are around people that cuss, it is easy to fall into it. Then it becomes a part of your vocabulary and for me, I have found it comes out in the worst moments. Like around Sean, and during closing arguments."

"Closing?"

"Oh, yeah, I said three or four curse words in a closing about a month ago and didn't even realize it until I sat down. Alonzo asked me if I had forgotten to bring Couth-Peter to court. I had no idea what he was talking about until he wrote the words down so I could read them. The fact that judge didn't hold me in contempt of court is a miracle."

"Did you quit cussing?"

"Not immediately, no. But, I have been trying to keep my tongue from letting profanity fly off of it," he admitted. "It also helps that I have been going to classes that have been helping me see things in a different light, as well."

"Classes?"

Peter waved the topic off. "It's a long story," he said. "Recognizing that we cuss way too much is healthy, though. What made you think about that?"

"Honestly?" she asked with a smile.

"Yes."

"I had Matthew 7:3 pop into my head."

Peter smiled. "Been reading the Good Book lately?"

"No," she admitted. "I have been working on this particular story and this is going to sound strange, but it's like God's working through the story to get my attention."

"That sounds like God."

"No, I am not talking about ... I mean," she stammered. "Let me ask you a question?"

"Go for it."

"Do you think that God can work through somebody that does not believe in him? Or, who doesn't believe in Jesus?"

Peter tilted his head to the side and furrowed his brow. It was the same look that he got whenever the opposing counsel was taking their questions down a path that he did not know how to defend. After a moment she saw the light bulb go off behind his expression and he leaned forward.

"I think that all things are possible for God. He is God. If he chooses to work through a believer then he can do so in any congregation or through any Christian and show his glory. If he chose to demonstrate his power through an unbeliever, then that would be even more awe-inspiring because he would be showing that unbeliever and all who were witnesses just how powerful he really is."

"Good argument, Counselor. Spoken like a true lawyer."

"Hey, I have my moments where I do not open up my mouth just to insert my foot."

CHAPTER FOURTEEN

C assandra half awoke to the smell of breakfast cooking and the sound of Sean laughing. She was too tired to drag herself out of bed and her mind was still checked-in to the Snooze Motel but she could have sworn that there were eggs being fried.

Just a dream, she thought and let her eyes roll back further into her head. She had a bunch of strange dreams the night before that she vaguely recalled. Peter brought Sean home and ended up staying the night. They had talked about God and Scripture for hours and she seemed to recall Peter told her about a class he had been attending. She thought that it was called...

"Now Is Here," she said and sat up.

The smell of breakfast and Sean's laughter was not a dream. Peter was there cooking breakfast and she had to think about how Sean might take this. Will he understand that his Daddy slept on the couch and that that does not mean we are back together? Oh, God.

Cassandra got out of bed and grabbed a robe to throw over her pajamas. She did not want Peter to get the wrong impression. It was then that she saw her phone was flashing. She picked it up and checked it at which point she realized that she was an hour late. It was a few minutes after nine and she was supposed to be at the office at eight for the meeting Hal intended to have on the future of the paper.

"Oh, crap," she said.

Her phone had several messages. Some from Hal, a bunch from Tanisha that were clearly prompted by Hal and then there was a few from a number that she did not recognize. She abandoned the robe and pajamas after she closed the door and threw on a pair of Capri and a short sleeved shirt. She didn't have time to do her hair so she threw it up into a ponytail and ran in to the bathroom to brush her teeth. She could not believe that she was an hour late.

The entire time that she brushed her teeth, she wondered why she had not heard her phone go off. When she finished, she called Hal and began to pace the floor as she slipped into her flip flops and attempted to remember where she left her bag.

"There you are," answered Hal. "Have you not read any of your messages?"

"I saw that you all messaged but I was in a mad dash to get out the door so that I could get there before eleven."

"Coming here?"

"Yes."

"Why?"

"The meeting that you were going to have at noon and I was hoping to speak with you before you got caught up with all that you have to do."

"The meeting is Monday, Cassandra. Today is Saturday. And, you really ought to read your messages."

"What?" she asked and checked the phone. Hal was right, though. "My schedule is all screwed up."

"It sounds like it. I got my days mixed up on vacation, too."

"So, what's going on?"

"I will give you the bad news first," he said. "Geoff blundered with Tanisha last night, which I am going to need you to fix somehow."

"How has he blundered?"

"Oh, no, that's something that you are going to have to talk to him about. I'm not getting in the middle of it."

"Hal, what did he do?"

"Cassandra, I am telling you as your boss that you are going to talk to him about it and if you have to, you will talk to her about it. There is a reason I have a policy that discourages dating among our staff."

"Wonderful, I feel like I am in the hot seat."

"You are and I expect that you will make sure that the problem gets resolved."

"Good news?"

"We printed papers today and the articles were edited and nothing fell apart in your absence."

"Are you trying to tell me that you can do just fine without me?"

"Yes and no. What I am telling you is that if you find that what you are doing now is more to your liking than editing, we will miss you but we will make it."

"Are you trying to get rid of me, Hal?"

"In no way am I trying to get rid of you. I would hate to lose you because you are an asset to this paper and I value you. However, I want to see you happy and doing what you love and enjoy."

"Thanks," said Cassandra.

The conversation ended with them both laughing and Cassandra checked her messages. Hal's were about what he already talked to her about so she then went on to check Tanisha's.

The first one read: *When u get this, call me. It's important.*

The second one read: *I'll b busy when u get these. FYI, ur boy's never gone out with a black woman. IJS.*

Cassandra smiled at the fact that Tanisha was now one of her many contacts that used 'IJS' to shorten 'I'm just saying' in text messages. She texted her back as soon as she read the second message with: Call me when you can.

She did not even want to think about what Geoff might have said or done that could have offended her. Tanisha was a professional woman that carried herself with a great deal of poise. Her demeanor was grateful and sweet at work and Cassandra had run into her a few times at the mall where she was just as delightful and kind. It was difficult for Cassandra to see her angry.

The same was true for Geoff, though. He was the kind of guy that would bend over backward and give the shirt off his back if it would help someone. He never got angry, even when he realized that the joke was on him, which it usually was; and for the most part he was a good sport. She hoped that whatever happened she could get them to smooth it over.

No longer needing to be at the office before noon, Cassandra decided to go ahead and take a shower before she made her way to the kitchen. She put on the same clothes that she had thrown on before and ran a brush through her hair before she set out. She found Sean sitting on one of the swivel stools eating an omelet covered with mustard and cheese and Peter sitting next to him eating a BLT.

"Good morning, guys," she said.

"Mom, Dad made breakfast and it is great. He puts peppers inside it like I like and there is all this cheese and the sweet mustard is marvelous."

Cassandra smiled and gave Sean a hug and reminded herself to not be awkward if he asked about his dad. She hoped that he wouldn't ask if his dad was going to live with them again. There was a limit to what she could handle and she was sure that God understood.

"I made you an omelet, too."

The third plate sat by the stove and the mere sight of the omelet made her stomach rumble and mouth water. "It smells wonderful."

"It sure does and it tastes even better, Mom," said Sean. "Guess what Dad and I are going to do today?"

"What is that, kiddo?"

"We are going to the Air and Space Museum!"

"That is fabulous, Sweetheart! How awesome is it that you get to go to the Air and Space Museum?"

"It's majorly out of this world."

Cassandra was elated that he was so excited. She wanted to go with them. She was tempted to call Doc and ask if he could wait to go back to the Pratt's until

later in the evening. Yet, she already knew the answer
to that question. Doc had been clear that they would be
gone between the hours of two o'clock and four, so if they
were going to set up all the equipment that needed to be
set up and investigate further, their time frame did not
allow for a later. They would have to go without her.

Cassandra sat down next to Sean and decided to be
happy that she could enjoy breakfast with her son. It was
a great break from the hectic rush of getting him ready
and out the door, all while getting ready and attempting
to get out the door, too. She did not remember when she
last had the time to sit down and eat breakfast with but
she knew that she wanted to do it more often.

When they were done, Peter offered to wash the dishes
and straighten up the mess he had made while Cassandra
got Sean cleaned up and ready to go. The topic of his
dad staying with them never once came up as she got
his clothes out and he selected what he wanted to wear.
That was a relief. She was not sure how she would answer
him if he did ask and hoped that the immediate decisions
before him were enough to keep his mind occupied.

The truth was that Peter had not been the man she
fell in love those many years ago for a long time. He
had stopped trying and had given up on working it out.
She still was not sure what had come between them or
what had stopped being between them that made their
relationship fall apart. She still loved him and there was
nothing in this world that could change that. Even if he
wanted to sign divorce papers, she knew that she could
not do it. He would have to drag her to her court and she
had grounds to divorce him, not the other way around.

What drove everyone crazy was that they were still married, even if they did not live together. Cassandra knew that aside from throwing the word divorce at each other once or twice, in frustration and in exhaustion, she was in no way serious about it. Nor was she prepared to throw their marriage away just yet. She wanted to believe that he could change and love her the way that she loved him regardless of how long it took him to change.

In the beginning he had tried to win her affection back and show her that they still had the romance that they had when they first got married. She knew that she had been too hurt at the time for it to have had any effect on her. But just when she was starting to think that she was falling in love with him again, he backed off and it all ended, leaving them where they were now.

"Mom, can I wear my comfy sandals?" asked Sean.

"Yes, you may."

"This is going to be out of this world! I will get to see rockets, and eat space food! We might even get to see Ben Ten!"

"Sweetie, I don't think Ben Ten is going to show up at the Air and Space Museum. He might, but don't get your hopes up."

"Of course he will be there, Mom. He is Ben Ten."

Cassandra wanted to laugh with the amount of enthusiasm that he had over Ben Ten being at the Air and Space Museum but she didn't want him to think that she was laughing at him. She also wasn't sure if he knew something that she didn't. She didn't want to tell him Ben Ten wouldn't be there if there was some sort of scheduled appearance that she was unaware of.

"Where did you hear that Ben Ten would be there?" she asked as she watched him put on his first sandal.

"Dad said that he is taking pictures there."

"That is too cool. Are you excited about seeing him and getting your picture taken?"

"Yes!"

Cassandra gave him a hug and a kiss on the cheek. "Go brush your teeth and then tell your dad that you're ready!"

Sean darted off for the bathroom as Cassandra made her way to the kitchen. Peter was scrubbing the skillet and looked to be almost finished when she walked over and started putting the plates in the dishwasher.

"Did he ask you any questions this morning?"

Peter laughed. "Aside from 'what's for breakfast dad' as he jumped on the couch? No. You?"

Cassandra shook her head. "What if he does?"

"We will deal with all of that if he brings it up," he said. "He's a smart kid. I think that he knows this morning isn't the norm."

"No. It's not. It was nice to get to sit down with him and eat breakfast, though. Thank you for cooking."

"You're welcome."

Before either of them could say anything else, Sean came barreling through the door. "I'm ready! I'm ready!"

"I guess we are off, then," said Peter.

Cassandra smiled and knelt down to give Sean a hug and a kiss. "Be good for your dad and don't forget to say thank you, yes, sir, and what else?"

"No thank you, no, sir, yes, ma'am and no, ma'am."

"That's right, Sweetheart. Good job."

Peter grabbed his keys off the counter and led Sean to the front door. As she watched her son follow his father, Cassandra realized that Sean was wearing the same sort of outfit, down to the sandals, as his dad. He even walked like him. They might have been separated but the amount of time that they got to spend together showed.

"Peter," she said as they opened the door and turned to wave goodbye. "Look at your son."

Peter looked down and studied Sean for a while without seeing what she saw. Then, he smiled and looked up with a grin. "We match."

"We do! We totally match! Wow!"

"That is amazing. Who picked out your clothes?" Peter asked as he ushered Sean out the door.

"Well, I did, of course."

With one last batch of waves, the door closed and ended the conversation on Cassandra's side. She had to laugh at Sean's words. He was right, though. She had pulled them out and he picked what he wanted to wear. And what he picked resembled what his father had on. She knew that she needed to think more about that but as she looked at the wall clock she realized that if she wasn't going to the office, she needed to get to the Refuge to help Doc load up the equipment.

CHAPTER FIFTEEN

Most of the equipment was already packed up into Doc's car when Cassandra arrived. The only thing left was a camera bag and to get in the car and go. She felt bad for not being there sooner to help but the drive took a lot longer than she had expected. Doc did not let that get in the way of his excitement, though. When she apologized, he just shrugged with a smile, pointed at the bag and continued making his sandwich.

"You can load the camera up."

"That doesn't seem fair. You loaded everything else."

"You're going to help unload it. Besides, I wanted it all in there a certain way."

"Tell me what it is that we are going to be doing?"

"We are going to tick off an entity, more than likely."

"Wait. We aren't going over there to tick whatever it is off, are we?"

"Not intentionally, no. That would be like challenging God to a wrestling match."

"There is a story where Jacob wrestled with an angel."

"How'd that work out for him?"

"If I remember correctly, he had a permanent limp afterward."

Doc brought the sandwich to a halt and stared at her over it. "Like I have a bum knee from sports in high school limp or I got hit by a car and no longer have much use for my leg sort of limp?"

"You are the one with the degree, you don't remember?"

"If I could remember everything I ever read, or studied, I'd have no need for the library."

Cassandra laughed. "Good answer. I don't remember either, but the Bible said limp."

"I really like not having a limp," said Doc with a cringe.

"You *are* afraid, aren't you?"

Doc sighed and opened his eyes wide as he nodded. "Well, yeah. If this *is* an angel, and the research suggests that it is, I don't want to tick it off too much. I value the flesh that I am in. It happens to be the only body that I have."

He was genuinely afraid of what the angel might do to him if it felt disrespected. She could see that clearly and wondered if he would even go back by the way the color drained from his face.

"You have faced all sorts of things, and even helped heal a boy that was possessed by an entity that a priest could not exorcise. Now you are afraid of an angel?"

"You don't understand. I've never run across an entity that does what this one has done. That is, if we believe the account of the angel throwing punches and so forth. The rest of the entities that I've helped with, I had to seek them out and discover them. It is different when an angel walks through you and says, 'Hi, pardon me, you seem lost. The *exit* is that way.'"

Cassandra could not hold back her laughter. "I'm sorry," she managed. "I mean…I…you…."

Doc stood in front of her with a sour look on his face for a moment and then eased into a smile as he had to admit to himself that it was funny. Cassandra was glad, too. Because to hear him say 'you seem lost' was worth the tears that had started to pour from her eyes.

"You said, 'Pardon me' and sounded like that guy talks on that commercial." Cassandra tried to manage but instead busted out laughing again.

"What?'" asked Doc, now laughing just as hard as she did.

The fit of laughter started to subside after a while and they both managed to get the hysterics under control. Cassandra had to wipe her eyes and blow her nose, which she was sure made her mascara run and seemed crude but Doc was in no better shape.

"That was too much," said Doc. "And it's not even really all that funny."

"Don't take us back into that, please," she asked. "And I don't know about you but to me, that was hilarious."

"I want to read the scripture you were talking about. And, why didn't you tell me about it during research?"

"I didn't think that it applied to what we were looking for."

"Man and an angel wrestle and God lets the angel put man in a limp producing figure-four, guess who wants to know about that?" he asked and walked over to the bookshelf.

Doc turned to the back of the Bible and looked at the reference section. He flipped a few pages in the index until he found what he was looking for and then turned the pages all the way to the front of the Bible. Cassandra watched as he read and saw that his face furrowed in concern. After a moment, he closed the Bible and took a deep breath before going into the room that Cassandra had never been in.

When he opened the door she was surprised to find that there were all sorts of statues in the room. Everywhere she looked in the bedroom, there were figures that she recognized and many she did not. One in particular that caught her attention was a sculpture of Jesus on the cross. Yet there were so many.

"I thought you had a lot of statuettes out here," said Cassandra as she stood in the doorway and pointed over her shoulder.

Doc looked back at her as he retrieved another Bible from the shelf. "What's wrong with my statues?"

"Nothing, if you like the museum décor," she said and found a hawk-statue that stood next to a mysterious mask done in various colors. "I don't think that I have ever met anyone who is as fascinated by mythology as you are."

"Are you judging me?"

"No. It's your place, decorate however you want. Can I ask you a serious question, though?"

"Ask away."

"What *do* you believe in?"

Doc closed the Bible on his finger and gave her question some thought. She watched as his eyes move around the room, lingering on this statue and that before they all swept across his entire field of vision. "I am not sure what I believe in, for me, to be honest."

"Okay, well there has to be something that you believe in. Start there. Do you believe in the afterlife?"

Doc nodded. "Yes, I have believed in the afterlife since I was young."

"Do you believe in heaven and hell?"

"From which belief system?"

"Just answer the question."

"How? I mean, almost all beliefs have a place where we stand before a particular deity or group of deities and are judged, after which we are then sent to wherever the deities judgment determines we should go. If I had to say precisely what I believed, I'd have to say that when we die we all stand accountable before some higher authority or host of higher powers, if you will and they then determine what to do with us."

"Do you believe that God has come to earth?"

"This is where my answers start to anger people."

"Do you believe that God has come to earth?"

"I don't believe that the higher authority *hasn't* come to earth."

"You really don't know what you believe in, do you?"

"Why can't I just believe in everything and live peacefully with everyone?"

"Everything? Really?"

"I know what you're going to say next," he said and raised his hands and the Bible.

"What?"

"That God does not want us to worship false gods."

"No, that was not it. I was going to say that wide is the path that leads to destruction," she admitted. "But that one is just as good."

Doc shook his head and went back to the Bible verse. She watched him read it and re-read it. After a few minutes of reading side notes and following the footnotes, he closed the Bible and put it back on the shelf. Then he just stood there and tapped his lips with his index finger.

"What?"

"I am suddenly seized, with great affection, to not have my hip dislocated from the socket."

"Hip? It's been too long since I have read that passage."

"Oh, and it would seem that not only did this man wrestle with this supernatural being, be it an angel or a man of extraordinary means, Jacob went on to say that by doing so he had seen God."

Cassandra thought that she remembered that part. "Like what you said, that some theorize angels are an extension of God?"

"In this case, it could lend merit to the idea. I just don't know if I want to go collect the empirical evidence and be broken up as a result."

"Have you considered that this could be God trying to get your attention?"

Doc laughed at that. "Now it's my time to say it. Really?"

"What if God has been working through you all this time, despite your denying him like Peter and doubting him like Thomas?"

"Nice analogy but I am sure that God has better things to do with his or her time than work through me.

I am nobody important and I am certainly not deity-attention worthy."

"Maybe not to most Gods but Christ might have something else to say that could surprise even you."

Doc looked at her and shook his head. "Now you're starting to sound like my mom and dad."

"Wait, they were Christians?"

"Yes, through and through. My father came to Christ, but he wasn't a run out and convert the world sort. Mom, though, her faith was just a part of who she always was. She used to tell me that she dealt with the patients that they lost at the hospital because she knew that God had a plan for them. God had a plan for everything, come to think about it" he said.

Cassandra wanted to ask him if he hoped to ever see them but felt that that would be insensitive. She decided to let the memory of his parents be and stepped back out of the doorway to allow him to pass through.

"Do you know what I have a difficult time with?"

"What?"

"If he loved them, then why did he take them? They never hurt anyone."

Cassandra did not have an answer. She didn't know what to say to him because no matter what she said, she doubted that he would hear her.

"Besides, there's an old legend, I think it's a Jewish one, because it was my grandfather who used to tell it to me, of a man who cursed Christ or God and was then forced to walk the earth," he said and shook his head. "It's been a long time since I've heard it. I just recall the fact that if you lash out at God, he doesn't forgive that."

Cassandra had never heard anything of the sort. She knew that if you blasphemed the Holy Spirit then there was no forgiveness. But how he could deny Christ from coming into his heart over a Jewish legend made no sense to her.

"Damien, he is a merciful God and a loving God. He forgives all our sins, even doubt, denial and getting mad at him."

Doc waved her off. "Let's not get into this right now. We have to decide what we are doing."

"We?"

"If I go, you're going, too, right?"

Cassandra shook her head. "I don't think so. In fact, I am pretty sure that I don't want anything to do with the Pratt house. If it is an angel, then the Bible says not to test God. I believe in God and I understand now that if I follow you, I am putting my faith in jeopardy."

"What about our agreement?"

"Certain things take a higher priority than agreements," she said. "I agreed to follow you and see if this is something that I wanted to help you write. I don't need to see anymore. I saw where I wanted to be today before I ever left my apartment and I assure you, it was not at the Pratt house and it in no way involved testing God."

Doc stared at her for a moment. "So, you're out?"

"Out."

"You're done with all of this just like that?" he asked.

"Some things, no matter how well intended they may be, do not line up with the life that I want to lead nor the example that I want to set for my son. I do not want to be mean, Doc, but there is not enough money or curiosity on this planet to make me want to continue on with this, whatever this turns out to be."

"I need you, though."

"No. What you need to do is pray and talk to God. Besides, who better to ask to not rip your hip out of socket than *him*?"

Cassandra turned on her heels and headed for the door. She was done with all of it. She loved God and saw that he was working in her life in ways that she didn't even understand yet. She had a good job and she loved the people that she worked with as much as she loved the work itself. She had people there that valued her as a co-worker and a friend; and regardless of what happened with the economy or what Hal chose to do with the newspaper she was not going to leave them when she still had an opportunity to make a difference.

She knew that she might be out of a job if Hal chose to sell. Yet, she also knew that she could find work that didn't test God. There was too much happening all at once for him not to be involved and if she waited for it to get any clearer, she feared that she would disappoint him.

She turned the door handle and pulled the door open. It was then that she felt moved to turn around and tell him what came to her right then.

"Doc, you really need to get out of here and live a little. I could tell you that Christ wants to be alive in you and that God is a living God, waiting on you to open up to his *grace*, but you're the type that has to know. You can't just take it on faith, can you?"

"It's not that simple."

"It's not that complicated," she said. "Just have faith in God, accept His *grace* and believe. Oh, and, one last thing, let the old gods of the old world go. They aren't real. They were created, in stories, by man to explain God's everyday miracles. If you spend your whole life trying to understand all of it, then you will miss out on the wonder God has given each of us, which is living life by his grace. Now, that's a marvel worth writing about!"

CHAPTER SIXTEEN

The Pratt house was staring at Doc. He knew that it was not the house but whatever entity was inside of it and it made him shiver in spite of the day's heat and the humidity. He wanted to run back to his car, throw it into drive and burn rubber out of there. He might have done that if his four-cylinder were capable of such a feat. The sad fact of the matter was that running to the car would only accomplish two things: provide the entity inside the house with a comical display of how terrified he was and prove that he did in fact need a new transmission.

He forced himself to go up the stairs and make the journey to the front door. Every step was a backfiring car away from running for his life and as aware of this as he was he knew he had to go in. He had to. As soon as Cassandra left, Doc knew that he had to continue on alone. He did not want to. Every shred of common sense told him to just leave and forget about the Pratts. The entity was good. There was no harm in a good entity. Let it be. It had nothing to do with him. He could just walk away.

Yet, as soon as his fears and concerns reinforced avoiding the place, something else, perhaps logic, perhaps understanding that the esoteric could not harm anyone unless the person allowed it to, he wasn't quite sure what the something was but it encouraged him to go.

All of that had been well and fine in the car. He had control in the car. The radio rocked out his favorite local station, the traffic gave him time to think as he sang along to the songs he did and didn't know. His voice was out of pitch and key as usual but he was having a good time. All the material he'd covered over the years and all the lectures he had listened to all shouted: it's just a belief and that is where the power is at, it has no power over you.

Yet, now, as he reached the door, all he'd ever learned meant nothing. He was not sure if it was his fear saying: If you come in, you're not leaving here; or if it was the entity inside the house. He had never encountered an entity that could hurt him. Until now he was not even sure that such a phenomenon was possible. Real or imagined, was it not his fear of uncertainty that made his hand tremble? Was he not allowing the possibility of an angel to become something more than what it was? If he let it have control, then it had control. Wasn't that what he had been taught?

Doc reached out, opened the door and rushed into the house. He ran into the foyer and swung the door back so that it shut behind him and then stood in the foyer for a long time. His heart raced, his breath came in deep near hyperventilating gasps and he waited for the wrath of God to knock him back through the door.

Nothing happened.

He opened his eyes. There was no bright light. No angel wreathed in the holy fire of God's wrath to smite him. He was alone in the foyer and from the sounds of the house it was just as empty as where he stood. He glanced around to make sure that he hadn't missed a hovering cherub and then made his way into the office. Nothing in there either. He made his way through the rest of the house and found nothing extraordinary or even out of the ordinary.

Once he was in the kitchen, he began to laugh at the absurd notion that God was going to have an angel waiting on him. He couldn't stop laughing at how preposterous the entire notion was. The God and not just any God, the All-Powerful, All-Present and All-Knowing God that created heaven and earth was going to take time out of his busy schedule to put an angel in his life. That was hilarious.

The clapping that came from behind him made him jump and spin around. As his mind attempted to make sense of the man that leaned against the kitchen counter, he felt embarrassed and angry that he did not announce himself.

"Mr. Pratt?"

"Are you serious?" the man asked with a laugh. "Mr. Pratt?"

"You are not supposed to be in here, I'll call the cops," he said as pulled out his cellphone.

The man smiled and then placed his hands on the counter nonchalant. "I love authority and it's been such a long time since I've had the privilege of speaking with an officer of the law."

Doc darted down the hall and tried to dial 911. Before he could finish pushing the buttons, the screen went blank and the hour glass began to circle on it. Of all the times for his phone to glitch on him, now was not the time. He looked up just in time to slam into the man from the kitchen.

"Oh, God!" he cried as he fell to the floor.

The man shook his head and extended his hand out to Doc. "Why do you all always do that? No matter how many times I hear it, I always hope that one of you will know the dissimilarity."

Doc thought he might have peed himself. He wasn't sure. His head was spinning from running into the guy or the wall. Once again, he wasn't sure. "I…uh…air…help," said Doc as he gasped.

"Oh, no, you're still hyperventilating? What about that whole inner-preparation-talk you did all the way to the front door?" asked the man as he handed him a brown paper bag. "Take this before you pass out."

Doc took the bag and put it to his lips. He closed his eyes and breathed, letting the bag crumple and expand. *Is this happening right now? Is this really happening right now?*

"Oh, yeah, this is happening. You are on the floor, breathing into a bag," said the man. "Calm down, relax. You're fine, I promise that I won't pull your hip out of socket so long as you don't make me."

Oh, God. Oh, God.

"Whether you say it aloud or think it, it still doesn't make it so, Damien."

He concentrated on his breathing and let the bag expand and contract. It took several moments before he got himself under control. During that time, he found that looking at the man was not as terrifying as it had been when he started to understand who he crashed into.

When he was able to stand the man extended his hand out to him again, and said with a sincere smile, "C'mon, take a hand of refuge for a change."

Doc reached up and took the man's hand and found that he was up on his feet without any effort. The man didn't strain, grunt or even flex a muscle in lifting him off the floor. It was unreal.

"You're an…" but the man waved him off before he could finish.

"I *am* sent me. That is what I am," he said. "No more, no less."

"Do I call you, I *am* sent me?"

The man shrugged. "I prefer to be called Meir."

"Meir?"

"Yes, but that's a long story, which has nothing to do with you. You can call me Ezer. Yeah, that's nice. He enjoys that a lot."

"I can call you Ezer? Wait, I am confused."

"That is Okay," said Ezer. "I haven't found one of you that has had it all figured out yet, anyway."

"This is not happening right now."

"You have got to stop saying that. I know that you're just so surprised and beside yourself in the amazement of the moment, but the things you all say sometimes…"

Doc felt very self-conscious about his words all of a sudden. "I didn't mean to…"

"I know and most important knows, too; however, consider how awful it would be for you right now had his son not come and paid it forward in grace? You, Mr. Doubt Him and Deny Him until you literally got knocked to the floor by the one he sent to you, still saying 'this isn't happening' after he sent his hand of refuge to pick you up? Do you know what he would have had to do to you before?"

Damien put a hand on his hip. "Sort of."

"Oh, no. Israel enjoyed that limp. It hurt but he loved God for it because he knew God and he knew God was merciful to him. You, you would have gotten hurt and not in the good teaching-you-a-lesson sort of way," said Ezer with a chuckle. "Don't get me wrong, it pains me to tell you that. However, were it not for Christ's actions, you would have been smote down and that's not to be confused with smitten, either. He would have taken you off the face of this planet with love, just not the smitten with you sort of love."

Damien shuddered. "All because I said..."

Ezer raised his hand and made Damien jump back. "Are you dense? Or did you not hear me the first time?" asked Ezer. "Let me explain this the easiest way that I know how. Do you have health insurance? Keep playing with God and you'll be using it."

Damien stepped back afraid. He didn't know what to think. His stomach was churning and he felt close to throwing up. There was no doubt in Damien that the being in front of him could smite him if he so desired. No sooner than he thought that, Ezer pointed to the ceiling and patted the back of his hand.

Damien backed up yet another step which made Ezer shake his head. "I'm sorry."

"Here we go. That right there tells me that you don't get it."

"Get what?"

"The salvation that God gave all of you, grace, and what it means to repent of your sins."

"I... uh..." stammered Damien as he felt ashamed and pained. The angel's words made him feel horrible and he could not express the agony that resulted as he remembered an old lesson he'd learned about salvation.

"For you all, though, when you remember, it hurts like it does right now and all the sin since hurts as you start to wallow in it because you forget that God loves you. You forget that Christ paid for your sins. You also forget that when you repent, I *am* is he who remembers your sin no more.

"It's all still in there, he sees, all you have ever learned," said Ezer with a smile. "He wants you to remember so you will know that it's true he works all things according to his purpose, even stubborn men, which by the way, he foresaw when he laid the foundations of the earth."

"I haven't..."

"He knows that you haven't sought after him in years but he never stopped calling out to you. He got you here, didn't he?"

"What do you mean?"

"I *am* is The Genius of all Geniuses. Nobody comes close to understanding what He has set in motion and through Christ all things are possible because even the boundaries of death and the very veil that separated you all from God is no longer an issue. Come here. Let me show you."

Damien followed Ezer into the nursery and watched the angel as he gestured to the crib. "Look at the baby."

"There…"

"…is a baby in the crib and he wants you to look at the infant-child."

Damien stepped over to the crib and looked down into it. Staring up at him were the sweetest and most wonderstruck eyes he had ever looked into. Nothing compared to how precious the baby was for there was no confusion in the child's eyes. There was just a smile and a chortle of mirth at having a face peering down into the crib.

"What's that he hears inside? Protect, defend, and do whatever it takes to be there for?" asked Ezer.

Damien nodded even though he knew that he did not put the feeling into thought. He didn't even bother to question how Ezer interpreted what he felt. God was involved and it was clear that there was no way to hide from God.

"The whole purpose of this particular job was to show you some things, Damien. This infant is how God sees all of you every time you repent and return to him. You're all as children to him as the Scriptures say but more specifically you all are newborns in his mercy and grace. All he wants is to protect you and help you get up on your feet so that you can walk with him. And, he will help you all when you need help so long as you put your full trust in him."

"I want to," admitted Damien.

"He knows. Otherwise he would not have sent me to remind you of whom he sent for you."

"I have even tried to do what they did for me by giving back."

"Damien, when your parents said that they wished they could have given more in life to you, so that you could give to those in your life, they weren't talking about money, or a specific degree, they were talking about time and love."

Damien just stared. "What?"

"Your parents love you. They always have and they always will. But as you already know, money is good for paying bills and enjoying life within the blessings that God grants you, beyond that it can become a root of evil. What they wanted to give you more of was time and love. That is what they wanted you to be able to give more of, as well."

"I don't understand."

"We're not finished yet," said Ezer. "Come on let's step out into the hall with this."

Damien stepped out into the hall and followed Ezer toward the kitchen. Ezer stopped him and made him turn around where he saw a man and a woman arguing. Their insults were cruel and abusive with every syllable. The woman attacked the man as the man attacked the woman and the fight continued until Damien could not take it anymore.

"Stop this!" Damien yelled over the ruckus.

Ezer motioned with his hand and made the man and woman disappear. "He thought that you'd never ask."

"What does that have to do with me?"

"Excellent question," Ezer said with a grimace. "Every day that you fail God by not living as an example of

Christ in your behavior and by not using your talents to reach others, which effects people whether you realize it or not, this is what you're promoting."

Damien failed to see how that could be. He didn't believe in hitting women and he would never hit a girlfriend or strike a woman with his fist. "How?"

"Simple, if you're not with Christ's example of love, then you're in opposition to him. His example was to do whatever he had to do for his bride to be, the Church. The opposite of that is the Adversary's way. Think of it like this, opposition is synonymous with…." Ezer pointed at Damien to give the answer.

"Disagreement?"

"Exactly, and disagreeing with his example leads to what you saw here. If you don't agree with how Christ treats his wife and follow him in his example, then you're saying that you know how to do it better. Who does that sound like?"

"The Adversary."

"He knew you would catch on quick."

Ezer motioned to the front of the house and Damien went without wondering what was in store. He was sure that it was going to be something that he did not understand which Ezer would make clear. When they arrived at the foyer, he saw that Mrs. Pratt was at her computer looking up passages for help in marriage and he could see that Mr. Pratt was in the room across the hall from her praying with the Bible in his hands.

"Do you understand this?"

Damien shook his head. "I can't say that I do."

"This is a family doing their very best to keep it together in Christ while the Adversary works at them from the outside. Do you understand why he sent her to you?"

"No."

"Because, this could be a family that you don't help with the message of Christ's grace, by being too stubborn and choosing to not walk in the light of the Lord," said Ezer. "You try to help people and there are those that you have and there are those that you have not. However, what he wants you to see is that no matter what you try to give back, if you do not have grace, your efforts and works are of no real importance to anyone except the few you assist and yourself. You can't help them." Ezer pointed to the Pratt's. "So, what treasures are you really storing up and where?"

"I don't understand."

"You will. God is certain of that."

"Hey, this is a lot like…"

Ezer shook his head. "Here he thought you were done trying to figure his plan out," he said and started laughing. "We aren't finished, just yet. There is one more thing that you have to see before God's done shoving the truth all up in your eye, for today."

Ezer motioned to the front door and Damien opened it. They stepped out into the late afternoon and Damien was surprised to find that they were not outside but inside a large room that had skylights. It took him a moment to understand where he was. He hadn't been there since he was a kid and the view was much different as an adult.

He turned around in a circle and discovered that he and Ezer were in the middle of the room. They had stepped out into the middle of one of the Air and Space Museum's massive chambers where a space shuttle was on display on one end and planes hung from the ceiling on the other. There were all sorts of people admiring the sights and taking in the plaques that chronicled the particular achievements on exhibition, too, which made Damien wonder if they could see him and Ezer.

"Faith the size of a mustard seed," said Ezer. "It can move mountains, or people. Even transform and hide their appearance in case you forgot what he did on the road to Emmaus."

Damien knew that Ezra's words were a direct answer to his question despite not remembering the Scripture that Ezer referred to. He did vaguely remember that Jesus changed his appearance and revealed himself to his disciples, but he thought that was outside the tomb.

"He revealed himself to Mary Magdalene at the tomb," said Ezer. "For an educated man, you've forgotten quite a bit. You'll have time to reacquaint yourself with the Word. For now, the Word wants you to pay attention to what is in front of you."

Damien did not back talk Ezer or attempt to argue with him. How could an angel that had access to your thoughts be argued with? He knew it was futile and did his best to train his focus on what was in front of him.

That was when it occurred to Damien that the woman holding the hand of the six or seven year old beside the shuttle was Cassandra. He assumed that the man who stooped down in front of the boy with the space MRE was the boy's father and her husband, neither of which she had mentioned. It gave his heart a pang to know that she hadn't revealed she had a family.

"You never asked and she wasn't there to talk about herself."

"Why are we here?"

"To the point I see," Ezer chuckled. "We are here so that you may witness the marvelous power of I *am* in all his glory."

"I don't need to see anymore. I know." Damien was cut short by Ezer smacking the back of his head and then jabbing his thumb into his ribs. It didn't hurt all that much and was more in the way a friend might joke around, but it took Damien by surprise.

"Two ears and one mouth," said Ezer as he shook his head. "He knew you would have needed no more than to slam into me. However, this is not for you, this is to glorify him and your witnessing this will perform a work of his in you. Ready?"

Damien nodded. "Ready."

"I *am* is the master of everything and Christ is the Love of I *am* brought into this world. We won't get into what this world did to God's love. He forgave you all and let that go only as the *most high's son* could. However, you all did not bring Christ into this world and you all did not deserve it. I *am* chose to do that because it pleased him and he loved you all and knew it was the only way for you to be reconciled to him. Don't try to think about that too long because your brain will never get the magnificence of it until you are with him."

Damien's eyes leaked onto his cheeks as Ezer's words tore through all of his rationale and ability to debate the finer points. With all of his intelligence and love for the world's philosophies, his heart could not reject the beauty of the angel's words.

"That's what he likes right there," said Ezer. "Let it sink in and take up residence in there." Ezer patted Damien on the chest with a compassionate expression.

"I never thought…"

"He knows. Imagine how Peter felt after he spent all that time with Christ and Christ told him he would deny Him three times. Christ still forgave him and reinstated Him. Think of all the disciples, they were there, they saw Him in action and they fell short when they were there to see everything unfold. There is a reason He said that blessed would be those who believed and had not seen."

Damien nodded and let the words settle inside his mind. It occurred to him that he was seeing. God let him be brought there to see what was in front of him. He saw Cassandra still, laughing with her son and husband and it put a smile on his face to think that she had said she knew where she would have rather been before she left the Refuge. He was sure that God wanted him to see that. Yet, there was so much more.

Most of the people who were there were tourists. A great many of them were not even speaking English as they stopped to look and read what the plaques said. So often, he forgot that he did not need to look farther than outside his own door to find the cultures he admired. And they were not in some thumb-worn book or a red-eye flight across the world they were right in front of him.

"You're starting to get it," said Ezer. "Only all of the people here are tourists because whether they are locals or from around the beautiful globe, everyone that walks through those doors is enjoying a service that they won't find at home."

"I…" began Damien.

"… will understand," said Ezer. "You're still missing why you are standing here."

"Tell me."

Ezer inclined his head. "I *am* does not need you to believe in him to work his will through you. He can heal what pleases him and fix what he desires. He is the Doctor of all Docs and the Repairer of all that needs Repaired. She is a testament to that because her faith needed to be strengthened and God used you to strengthen her and make her see that she had lost her way. That was not your plan. That was his plan."

"Wait, she walked out and rejected my offer over her faith in God."

"That was what God wanted so that his plan for her could be done. She heeded the Spirit he gave to her and should she continue to do so, she will know the rewards God has in store for her. The same goes for you."

"It's hard to—"

"Believe that the faithful can forget whom they serve?' Where did leave that mirror?"

Damien bowed his head as Ezer checked around for a mirror that was not there. However, for an angel of the Lord, Damien was sure that he could produce one out of thin air.

"I see," said Damien. "I get it."

"He knows you do," said Ezer. "On the mirror part, at least"

"At least?" asked Doc.

"As God's plan unfolds and his *truth*, *word*, and *love* spread to every area of your life, you'll get more. That's how he works in all of you."

"What now?"

"That's up to where your faith or lack thereof leads you, Damien. Your free will gives you the choice of which to follow: your own will or his. His will has many things in store for you. Your will leads you down a path that puts you in your own way. Which will you choose?"

"I choose his."

Ezer nodded. "Then follow the Spirit that he sent to all who serve him."

CHAPTER SEVENTEEN

Cassandra sat down in the chair next to the hospital bed and looked at Doc. She thought that there was a slight smile at the corner of his lips, but she couldn't be sure. At this point, nobody was sure of anything. The doctors couldn't tell her what was wrong because she was not related to him; and the nurses had two separate theories on what could have happened. One was that he had suffered an ischemic stroke which resulted in the concussion when he fell. The other was that he may have had a seizure which caused the concussion when he fell.

Either way, Cassandra prayed that he would recover. She could not believe that she was the last person to see him; or that had she stayed a few minutes longer, she could have done something for him. She knew that she had to trust in God, but she hoped that he would give him a chance to accept Christ, at least.

The door opened to the hospital room and Cassandra was glad to see Father Mallory come in. The older priest looked concerned and the worry showed under his eyes. Cassandra got up and extended out her hand as she smiled.

"It's a pleasure to see you again, Father."

Father Mallory gave her a quizzical look. "Forgive me, Dear, I am not as good with faces as I used to be and nowhere near as good with names."

"I met you at Doc's, we had coffee?"

"Oh," said the priest. "I am sorry. It's been quite a while since I've drank coffee. You have to pardon the forgetfulness of an old man."

Cassandra stared at the priest. She almost started to remind him that it had not been but a couple weeks ago before she decided to let it go. For all she knew he might have been senile and she was not sure how it would help to correct him. Even if he wasn't senile, a couple weeks without coffee and the number of people he encountered might have caused him to just forget.

"It is okay, how are the Pratt's?"

Father Mallory stared at her for a moment and then looked at Doc. "How do you know about them?"

Cassandra knew now that his memory was going. She saw the same thing happen with Peter's uncle. It was sad. "You don't remember the conversation we all had? Samantha Pratt? You, Doc, and I over at the Refuge's pool house?"

Genuine surprise crossed Father Mallory's face. "I only found out about Samantha Pratt the other day when I discovered him lying in the floor. I haven't had a chance to tell him."

Cassandra was confused. What about the house they had gone to? The woman they met? She had spoken to the priest and gone to Starbucks with him. What was he trying to pull here? Cassandra was not sure but what she was certain about was that it was a bad time to be playing jokes.

"Father, perhaps you do not recall but it was just the other week."

Father Mallory shook his head. "I am sorry, I think that you must have me confused... the record of Samantha Pratt's family was just discovered in the rectory, in an old family Bible. I thought that Doc would like to know that he has a great-grandmother that is still alive so I stopped by to tell him. Beyond that, I have no idea what you are talking about."

Cassandra looked into the kind old eyes of the priest. There was no deception in them. He was just as sweet and compassionate as he could be and he had no reason to deny introducing her and Doc to Samantha Pratt. Come to think of it, we only ever met Samantha Pratt. Even at the house, it was only her and we never saw a child or a husband.

Cassandra shuddered. "I have to go."

"Have I upset you?"

"No," she said. "I just have something I need to do."

Cassandra left the room and headed out of the hospital. This was all too much. Her mind could not process what was going on. The whole reason she went back to the Refuge was because Doc wasn't answering his cell phone and she felt that it was important to let him know that his check had never posted to her account. Now she had to wonder if he had ever written a check to begin with and if he had what had it been for?

Every step that Cassandra took was one where she tried to clear her head and make sense of what the priest just told her. She had talked to him over coffee. She knew she had. He even told her that he had taken a vow not to ever talk about what happened with Doc openly and that if they were talking about coffee instead of Doc that coffee was a force to be reckoned with even if it wasn't in his traditional coffee cup. What was all of that?

As Cassandra tried to understand and make sense of what was going on, she made it to her car and got in. Before she realized it, she had started the car and driven across town to park her car in front of the Pratt house. The house was there and as sure as she was sitting in front of it, it was saved in her GPS from when she couldn't find it and had to have Doc give her directions over the phone to it.

"I'm not crazy."

Cassandra got out of the car and headed up the sidewalk to the front door. She rang the doorbell and waited for a long while before the door finally opened. A woman about her own age pushed the screen door open and gave her a polite smile as she held a two year old boy in her arms. There was no way to confuse Mrs. Pratt with the woman in front of her. Mrs. Pratt was definitely Caucasian where the woman in front of her was African American.

"I'm sorry but I'm not interested in buying anything," she said.

Cassandra noticed the No Solicitors sign on the door and was glad that the woman wasn't mean about not reading the sign. "I'm so sorry to bother you. Is there a Mrs. Pratt here by chance?"

The woman shook her head. "I hope not or my husband will have some explaining to do when he gets home from work. I think there is a younger couple named Pratt down the street, though."

"This woman would be about our age, she's white, with a baby girl."

The woman shook her head. "The Pratt's I'm thinking of wouldn't be who you're looking for either, then. She's Asian but he's white. No kids, though."

Cassandra shook her head. "No. I'm sorry to have bothered you."

"Not a problem."

Cassandra walked back out to her car in a daze. She got in the vehicle and tried to make sense of how she could have had the address in the GPS if she and Doc had not visited Mrs. Pratt at the house. It was as if she had imagined the whole experience. There was no way. She knew she had been there. She walked up those steps and she went into that house where Doc claimed that an angel walked through him and not in so many words the angel told them to leave.

Cassandra pulled out her cell phone and dialed Hal. "Hey, it's me, I have a question?"

"I already told you that we aren't going to sell the paper; and for the umpteenth time, no, it's not something I'll change my mind on," he said with a laugh.

"Thank you for the umpteenth time but I have a different question," she said and grinned. "I never discussed my meet with Doc at the Refuge with you did I?"

"No. Why?"

"Hal, I think I am going crazy."

"Why is that?"

"Because, I ran into someone who doesn't remember ever talking to me and a house that I visited, with Doc, turns out to not be a house that I visited."

"Hmm. Sure it was the same person and house?"

"Oh, there's about ninety-nine percent certainty. Although, I will have to talk to Doc when he wakes up just to make sure that I am not mistaken."

"Let me know how that works out," said Hal. "You know you still have five more days before you have to be back in to the office, right?"

"Yep."

"Okay, unless there is a major issue, I expect to talk to you then because some of us have a lot of work to do."

Cassandra laughed. "Hey, you work?"

"And, I thought you were getting right with God? Isn't there somewhere in the Bible that says that you have to give unto your boss what is rightfully your bosses?"

"Hey, we both know that I joke and if it hurts your feeling..." she laughed.

"No, it doesn't; but seriously, enjoy your time off and take this time to figure out what you're going to do," he said and let his words trail off.

"I already told you I am not going anywhere."

"No. Not about work, about what your trip to the Museum brought up for you, with Peter."

"I know what you meant."

"I figured you did. And, hey, I know that I said you should have divorced him a long time ago but if you still love him and you think that he won't hurt you again..."

Cassandra knew that was Hal's way of saying he would support her decision regardless of what he thought. All she could do was smile and thank him for being a good boss and a great friend. He played it off as only Hal could and then he remembered that he had a stack of work in front of him.

After they hung up, Cassandra took one last look at the house. She did not understand what was going on. Had Doc orchestrated a prank? Or was the simplest answer the one that defied what any other reasonable person would come up with?

"Huh," she said. Then something occurred to her and she pulled out her cell phone.

"Hey, Sis," answered Laney after a few rings.

"Hey, with everything that's been going on, this hasn't come up in a while but I wanted to know, whatever happened to that ghost of yours?"

"I don't know. I guess our prayers worked. He hasn't been around."

"Huh," said Cassandra again as she looked at the house. "Praise God."

CHAPTER EIGHTEEN

Cassandra had no idea what to expect as she looked down and checked the address on the paper. Excitement replaced her nervousness as the cab came to a halt and she got out. Her elation was so great that she almost forgot to pay the cab driver who smiled at her and blessed her for the tip.

As the cab drove off, she checked the address once again and looked up at the building. She was sure that she had to do this. Everything that God had going on in her life had brought her to this moment. And where she had questions before about what she should do next, the pastor at Isaac and Eisha's church had made it clear to her: Let no man separate what God has joined together.

He also helped her realize that whatever God's purpose was for Doc coming into her life, it had been fulfilled. God had demonstrated as much by moving Doc to another hospital while she was at the Pratt's house. She could not believe that he had been moved or that they would not tell her to which hospital but his will was done. That much she knew for sure.

She had gone back to the Refuge several times in the hope that Doc would be there. Each time she discovered that the pool house was as it had been the day that he went to the hospital. Unlocked and full of his stuff but no sign of Doc. She was not sure if he was still asleep in a hospital bed somewhere or if he had woke up and gone somewhere to make sense of his experience. He was just not there.

Louise had no idea where he was, either; and she expressed the most genuine concern for him. It not only surprised Cassandra, it also made her well up when she saw the hint of tears in the southern lady's eyes. Her tears could not be held back as she shared that she had a prayer chain going clear to Florida for his well-being. Together, they prayed for him and Cassandra saw that her first impression of Louise had been so wrong.

Before Oscar left the Refuge to start his new life and job, he told her that he had hoped to enjoy one of the send-offs that Doc gave to his friends before they left the Refuge. There was a hint of tears in the older black man's eyes as he smiled and admitted that if God willed it, he'd have Doc over to share a meal. He just hoped that wherever Doc was, he was okay.

Cassandra shook her head and smiled. She stared up at the building and started to laugh with all the joy and hope that God blessed her with. There was just one last thing that she had to do before she went in. She pulled out her cell phone and texted Eisha, Laney and Hal.

I'm here. Thank u all for being there 4 me! Love u guys!

She looked at the words on the screen and fought back tears of joy before she pressed send.

Cassandra stuffed the phone into her pocket and went into the building. She went to the front desk and asked where the banquet hall was, and thanked the man for his directions. Her destination was easy enough to find. All she had to do was go right and then walk straight up the hall to the double doors at the end of the corridor.

She opened the door and found that the people inside had just started to take to their seats. She glanced around the room and waved at Isaac before her eyes found Peter's. He smiled and got up to meet her at the door.

"I am so happy that you're here."

"Me, too."

"Let me introduce you to everyone," he said and turned around. "Everyone, this is Cassandra, my wife. Cassandra, this is everyone at Here and Now."

Cassandra waved. "Hi."

The group waved and everyone got up to shake Cassandra's hand.

"It is amazing that you are here and you're choosing to take this journey with Peter," said Isaac as he got his chance to hug Cassandra.

She hugged him back. "You and Eisha could have told me he missed me."

"We could have but God works out all things according to his timeline, not ours or anyone else's."

When the introductions were done and she had shaken everyone's hand, Cassandra sat down next to Peter. She still was not sure what the class was about. She knew what it was called and that the group was made up of Christians but beyond that she was trusting in Peter, as well as Isaac and Eisha.

"It looks like all of us are here," said Martin. "Since we have Cassandra here with us, I'd like to take a minute to share what this group is about. If we are missing anyone, it will also give them some time to get here. Okay? Everyone in agreement with that?" The group applauded and each member gave their clear approval.

"Excellent! Here and Now is a Christian group that's made up of various denominations. We have ex-Catholics who aren't sure what church is right for them. We have Baptists who used to be Methodists. We have Methodists that were raised up in the Synagogue. And there's a few of us who used to be either atheist or agnostic.

"We choose to meet here because it's neutral ground and we can focus on what we have in common rather than what our denominations differ on. What do we have in common?"

"Our Friend and Redeemer, Christ Jesus!"

"That's awesome! Somebody else want to take over?"

A woman whose name Cassandra believed was Ellen spoke up. "We discuss pretty much everything. If you are easily embarrassed, we try to apologize in advance. We get pretty ridiculous over Jesus. We love him. We think that everyone should just adore what He did for all of us. And even if someone doesn't believe in Jesus, we still love and accept them because, well, you know that He would."

"Should we tell her what our motto is?" asked Peter.

"Fantastic idea," said Martin. "Go ahead, you should have that honor."

"Our motto is: 'God's Love is today and every day, no matter where we are.'"

Cassandra smiled at Peter. "You have been coming to a God group?"

Peter nodded. "When you feel you're losing everything and your life is upside down, you have to do something. Denominational traditions aside, Christ is the only forgiving God there is. I needed His forgiveness and I need yours. I'm sorry, Cassandra."

Cassandra hugged Peter and enjoyed every second that he hugged her back. God was amazing. For the first time in their marriage, she felt as though God had been given full control. She was thankful to him for how he helped Peter and her both by opening their eyes to how he wanted their marriage to be.

"I forgive you," she said into his neck.

The applause in the room reminded Cassandra and Peter that they were not alone. They smiled at each other and let the people around them applaud, laugh, and talk. Neither of them wanted to take their eyes off each other. Not right then. Especially not when God was bestowing a miracle of grace.

EPILOGUE

"Uncle Isaac, why doesn't everyone go to Church?" asked Sean as he looked up from beside the van.

"Some do not go to Church because they believe that where there are two or three gathered, Jesus Christ is with them and they're serving the Lord. There are others who believe in God yet they believe in Christ differently than we do and they have a different interpretation of the Scripture."

Sean's brow furrowed. "Oh. How do they believe different?"

"Some people don't believe that Jesus died for them, others believe that he was not God in the Flesh."

"They don't believe? How can they not believe in the Lord?"

Isaac smiled and pointed down at Sean as Chris got out of the van. "He's got the conviction of the Lord."

"He's at the right place, then," said Chris as he shut the van door.

"Uncle Chris, did you know that there are people who do not believe in the Lord? Have they not been told about Him?"

Chris scratched his head in amazement at the tone of Sean's voice. "Huh," he said, and smiled. "This is a conversation that I am sure your father would prefer to have with you."

"How can they not believe in the Lord?"

"Doesn't believe?" asked Kyle as the van door opened.

Chris helped his son out of the van and Isaac looked to the car parked in front of them. "Peter, we have an excellent topic you're missing out on over here."

"Yeah, the Spirit of God is moving through the parking lot; you better hurry."

"There are people who haven't accepted the Lord," said Sean to Kyle.

"That's why God made Church," responded Kyle.

Peter arrived just as Kyle said Church and he turned to Isaac. "What are they talking about?"

"Sean asked why some people do not go to Church," said Isaac. "I told him what we already discussed at group."

Peter knelt down in front of his son. "Uncle Isaac is right, not everyone goes to Church but that does not mean they are bad people or believe in Christ any less."

"What about the ones who don't believe? Why don't they, he is our Lord?"

"There are some that do not believe he came and died for our sins. There are others who do not believe he rose from the tomb; they claim that his resurrection never happened."

Sean shook his head confused. "How can they believe that his resurrection never happened?"

"They have a different belief than we do," said Peter. "As for us and our house…?"

"We will serve the Lord."

"That is right. What do we do for them?"

"We pray for them and hope that God will open their hearts."

Peter nodded overjoyed and Sean took his father's hand as the rest of the group began to make their way towards the church. Friend's waved and stopped to talk to them as they all began to realize that the power outage from the previous night was going to make seating for the Sunday service a lot more interesting.

"Praise God," said Isaac. "I didn't know He had this many attending."

"You all may have to stand," said one of the friends.

"Amen to that said," said Laney.

"I third that," said Eisha. "Women and children get seats first."

"I have no problem standing, how about you all?" asked Peter.

The men all agreed that they would have no problem standing and made their way up to the church doors. As they walked in, Peter greeted and spoke with one of the men he knew from court. Sean stood beside his father for a minute and watched before he made his way over to one of the other greeters.

"Hi, we couldn't come to Church last night. I know I don't know you," he said and extended his hand. "My name is Sean. That's my dad and mom over there."

"Hi, Sean," said the man with a smile. "My name is Damien. Welcome to the Sunday service."

"Did you know that not everyone knows the Lord? And some people even believe that he never rose from the tomb?"

"I know," said Damien. "That is not what you believe, though is it?"

Sean shook his head. "How can someone believe that Jesus never rose from the tomb?"

"They choose not to."

"They choose?"

Damien nodded. "Yes, it is their choice to believe or not."

"I thought everyone believed in Jesus. My dad says that our house will serve the Lord, even if others don't. Mr. Da—?"

"Damien."

Cassandra stepped forward to retrieve her son and smiled at the greeter before she recognized who he was. Her jaw dropped when she realized and her eyes widened in shock. Damien smiled at her as she stood there searching for words.

"Mr. Damien, you don't believe that Jesus never rose from the tomb, do you?"

"I believe that Jesus rose from the tomb. Do you know what else I believe?" he asked as he gave Cassandra a wink.

"What?"

"I believe that God can make the biggest doubters believe in Jesus. Do you know how?"

"Because God can do anything?"

Damien nodded as Peter stepped forward to join his wife and son. Rather than let Peter interrupt the exchange, she put a hand on her husband's arm and gave him a look that he understood meant wait.

"That's right, God can do anything," answered Damien. "He even has the power to do what others will swear *never* happened."

"Hey, my mom says that," said Sean as he looked up and smiled.

"Peter this is…"

"Damien Kaufler," he said as he extended his hand.

"Damien this is my husband, Peter O'Neal."

Peter shook his hand. "It's nice to finally meet you. She's wondered what happened to you."

Damien smiled. "God happened."

CPSIA information can be obtained at www.ICGtesting.com
Printed in the USA
LVOW10s1402200514

386597LV00012B/122/P

9 781627 468510